THARKI

INDORI ISHQ

THARKI
INDORI ISHQ

KUNAL MARATHE

Leadstart

ISBN: 978-93-5458-172-4

First Published in 2017
Cover design: Amol Karambe
Layouts: Kshitij Dhawale, Leadstart
Editing contribution (2017 Edition): Kritika Sharma & Aditya Joshi

Published in India 2021 by
Leadstart
A Division of One Point Six Technologies Pvt Ltd
119-123, Building J2, Shram Seva Premises
Wadala (East), Mumbai 400 022, Maharashtra, INDIA
T + 91 96 99933000 **E** info@leadstartcorp.com
W www.leadstartcorp.com

Dedicated to

*Anyone who has ever fallen in true love**

**and got screwed*

ABOUT THE AUTHOR

Hailing from the city addicted to poha and jalebi—Indore—KUNAL MARATHE is a novelist and screenwriter living in the paradise of vada pav—Mumbai. After starting his career in Hospitality Industry and then spending significant years in Publishing and Book Marketing, he is now a full-time writer in Bollywood.

Relatively new in the Film Industry, Kunal has written web shows and films for some reputed Production Houses and Directors. The MX Original Show INDORI ISHQ is his first release and is based on this book.

SPECIAL THANKS TO

Sunir Kheterpal
for giving this book a new lease of life

ACKNOWLEDGEMENTS

THARKI would have been lost in piles of hundreds and thousands of novels out there had it not been made into a web show—Indori Ishq. Thanks to the brilliant team at MX Player—Amrita Goswami, Brijesh Tanna, Gautam Talwar and Tejpal Singh Rawat—who showed faith in this book and made a web show out of it. Samit Kakkad [Director of Indori Ishq], Amit Agarwal and Takesh Singh for being a part of this journey from book to screen.

Malini Nair, Trupti Sawardekar and Jayati Sarkar of Leadstart Publishing for republishing this book.

One of my closest friends who is no less than a brother, Amol Karambe, for always believing in my projects. Shilpa Pitroda—a talented writer—for reading various drafts of this book and giving valuable feedback.

Finally, many thanks to my parents for tolerating a mostly disappointing child and never disowning me!

PROLOGUE

'What's troubling you at this time of night?' Sub Inspector Baldev Mishra—as written on his name tag—asked in a disinterested tone as I took seat in a police station. A giant wall clock above the logo of Madhya Pradesh Police indicated that it was 3:10 a.m.

'I want to lodge an FIR.' I looked up morose, as if life had been drained out of me. Totally overpowered by alcohol, I tried my best to look sober.

'FIR for?'

'If a person promises to marry someone, they have physical relationship, and then that person cheats . . . and breaks the promise—what charges can be imposed on that person?' I asked hesitantly.

'Cheating, sexual exploitation, even rape—depending on certain factors,' the otherwise disinterested cop said with an unexpected attention and opened a thick, nearly torn register. 'Where is the victim? Let us take *her* statement and we will arrest the culprit immediately.'

'Actually, sir . . .' I said, 'the victim is not *her*. *He* is a man . . . It is me.'

Mishra looked confused. His facial expressions showed he tried to understand but failed miserably.

'Come again?' He bent closer to me.

'I was in relationship with this girl for long. We were committed to each other and were about to get married. We even had sex—many times. But then, she cheated on me for another guy and left me.'

'And you want me to lodge an FIR against this girl?' Mishra asked raising an eyebrow. 'FIR for rape?'

'Yes.' I nodded.

'Get up,' he said. There was a sudden change in his tone. It was far from polite.

'A-anything wrong, sir?' I faltered.

'First get up,' he roared this time and walked towards me.

'What is the problem, sir?' I stood up, confused.

'*Saale chutiye,*' he yelled with a power-packed slap on my face. 'What do you think we are here for? To listen to your nonsense?' he screamed again. 'Get out of here.'

And I was thrown out of the police station.

2008

TARA

CHAPTER 1

Baat uss daur ki hai jab mobile phones ne landline ki aur CDs ne cassettes ki leni shuru kar di thi. Google ke Orkut par Zuckerberg kaa Facebook dhire-dhire chadhane laga tha aur Yahoo Messenger ke din kisi budhe hote porn star ke career ki tarah khatam hone ko aa rahe the. Kutte-billiyon ke filter waali selfies se maanav jaati koson dur thi, aur Internet par videos ke naam par mujre kaa nanga naach nahin hua karta tha. Nokia ke extra-strong dabbe handset industry par raj kar rahe the, aur topi pehna ek singer apni naak ke surroor se music industry mein aag mutt raha tha.

Wait. Sorry. I had totally forgotten this is an English book. Forgive me, please. Actually it is human nature to shift to the mother tongue when lost in pool of memories—good or bad, does not matter.

Speaking of mother tongues, I had two. Hindi and Marathi. I belonged to a Maharashtrian family but was born and brought up in Madhya Pradesh. At home, I spoke Marathi. Stepping out, it was Hindi all around. Subsequently, I embraced both the melodious languages as my mother tongues.

With two sisters, I was the youngest of the siblings and undoubtedly Mom's favourite child. Dad, however, seemed more inclined towards the sisters—perhaps because he foresaw I was about to disappoint him a lot in near future.

Mine was a typical middle-class family in Indore—a fascinatingly colourful city in Central India known for its tempting delicacies, vivid religious festivities, gloriously captivating history, and enormous cultural heritage.

Though our family survived on the bare minimum and money was always a concern for us, my parents never compromised on education and spent most of their earnings on providing the best possible education to their children. I remember not having a cable connection at home for years during childhood but still studied in an English medium school—something uncommon for someone belonging to a lower middle-class family.

After my upper primary schooling, Mom and Dad went a step ahead and enrolled me in an extremely expensive school of the city—one of those meant for rich kids—and hoped their son would excel in academics.

Their son, however, had other priorities.

~

TARA. I moved the sharp needle of geometry compass like an artist, carving the name on my desk—last bench of fourth row, my usual seat in classroom. And when someone at the age of eighteen scribbles a name with no reason, even the dumbest dumbfuck on this planet can tell it is because of a thing called *love*.

Our Chemistry teacher was busy scribbling alien looking symbols on the blackboard, forty odd students were taking notes like programmed robots, and I—without giving another fuck about academics—was lost in Tara Shrivastav.

She sat six benches away from me, her almond-shaped eyes stuck on the blackboard. The simple yet elegant ring on her nose, the gorgeous dimple on her chubby cheek, the strands of curly hair escaping her ponytail—they were hypnotizing.

'Oye Romeo. Agar sirf taadane se ladki patt jaati naa toh har chutiya bagal mein girlfriend lekar ghumta.' Hari dragged me out of dream world. He was my best friend in school—unfortunately.

I avoided him and pretended to take notes.

'What's so special about Tara? Our school is full of chicks, you should explore other options as well,' he suggested, probably the hundredth time. It was his usual rant.

I often wondered if he too had a secret crush on Tara!

'I love her. That makes her special,' I hissed, barely looking at him.

'Reason?' he asked. The teacher shot an angry glance at us.

'True love is beyond reasons. If you love someone for a reason—the love ends with the reason,' I recited my love-*mantra* after the teacher resumed her scribbling. I was a philosophical ass since childhood.

'Okay, *Mr. True Lover,* but when will you propose to her—after she makes a baby with someone else?' Hari said.

My blood began to boil. I felt disgusted with the thought of Tara making a baby with someone else. *The baby should be mine*—I told myself.

'Today I will . . .' I muttered.

'You have been saying this for months,' Hari reminded me.

'I swear I will propose to her today,' I assured, resting my head on the desk, and I was back to the staring session. Tara smiled while talking to her desk partner, and my heart skipped a beat.

'Don't you think Tara is a little fat?' Hari spoke again. Keeping quiet and not vomiting some useless shit was next to impossible for him.

'She is chubby,' I fired.

'Just the same.'

'Chubby—not fat. She is chubby.'

'Fat or chubby, what's the bloody difference?'

'Your mom is fat. Sangeeta Ma'am is chubby.' Finally, my irritation got the best of me. Sangeeta Ma'am, by the way, was our Chemistry teacher.

'*Gaand mara*,' he barked, turning some heads in our direction.

I was once again lost in the eternal beauty of my sweetheart—Tara. She was concentrating on the blackboard. I was concentrating on her. For me, she was everything. For her, I was just another classmate.

'You should check her best friend, Anuja. She is cute—and slim,' Hari started again.

God! He was such a pain in the ass.

'Dogs go for bones. Tigers prefer flesh,' I put forward another mindboggling, mouth-shutting dialogue and winked. I knew I had won the argument.

Schooldays! After you grow up and face the brutal world out there—where every motherfucker you meet is looking for a chance to fuck you in one way or another—you realize that your schooldays were like an orgasm that lasted for years.

~

'Are you sure it's the right time?' I asked Hari one last time as we stood outside our classroom with our heads peeking inside, looking at Tara who was alone in there. She was perhaps making notes in the free period. And I was *almost* prepared to propose to her.

I was nervous.

Back then, I was hopelessly shy around girls. I was one of those weird boys who would speak like a politician on stage but go mute in front of a beautiful girl.

'I will kick you in the balls,' Hari lashed out. 'This is your last chance. Schooldays are almost over. And if you really don't want to lose her—get your ass in there and propose to her.' He pushed me forward.

'Alright then . . .' I muttered, suddenly getting nervous about my looks, my appearance and even my existence! I quickly opened the top two buttons of my shirt and removed the tie—I hated it. Tucking in my loose shirt, I scrubbed my shoes against my pants to make them shine. After smoothing my hair with fingers, I checked my dusky face in windowpanes. I was looking okayish. With an above average height and a lean body, I belonged to that category of boys who are neither termed too handsome nor ugly.

'Pehle beauty parlour ho aayein, chutiye?' Hari scoffed, staring at me.

I shook my head in negative, took a deep breath and entered the classroom.

My words came slow, steady, and cautious as I took a seat next to Tara. 'Making notes?'

'Yes.' She nodded in affirmation. She did not even lift her face to look up at me.

I stared at her, studying her face, her eyes, her nose pin, her hair—everything about her. She was simply gorgeous. With every passing moment, I was falling in love with her over and over again. I did not even realize when I grabbed her hand.

She pulled it back immediately.

Wrong move.

'I love you, Tara,' the words just blurted out of my mouth.

'What . . .!' She dropped her pen in shock. She was definitely taken aback. Her tone was a little high-pitched. She looked into my eyes for a fraction of a second, and then, her eyes lowered. Her lips curled once, as if she were about to say something, but she stopped. I desperately wanted to take her in my arms and kiss those perfect lips.

'Our schooldays are to be over soon, and I have decided to join Merchant Navy after this. I will have to shift to Mumbai to do B.Sc. in Nautical Science,' I told her. 'But before I go, I want to tell you that you are the one I want to spend my life with.'

It may sound a bit old-fashioned—and stupid—but I proposed to her for marriage in the twelfth standard—and I meant it. I was a totally different person back then. I completely believed in the *one love whole life* theory. Or perhaps, I did not know that life is actually quite different from those romantic Bollywood movies in which a guy falls in love with a girl and then they remain together forever!

She did not reply.

'I love you, Tara,' I spoke again.

No answer, yet again.

A piece of chalk came to me like a missile and hit my face. I looked for the source of it and found Hari standing at the door. *Give her the gift*—he said in signs.

It reminded me of the gift that was waiting in my schoolbag. I had bought it for Tara weeks ago—but had not gathered the courage to give it to her until that day. I quickly pulled it out of my bag and presented it to her. Wrapped in beautiful laces was a heart-shaped scrapbook. 'This is for you,' I offered, lovingly.

'Thanks,' she finally spoke and carefully kept my gift in her bag.

'What's your a-a-answer, Tara?' Out of the blue, I felt like I was having a spasm in my tongue and a strong jolt of headache hit me—like a migraine. Everything sort of started to spin and my vision began to blur.

I grabbed Tara by her shoulder as firmly as possible. I knew I was going to fall and did not want it to happen on my perfect day.

'What happened?' she yelled, worriedly. 'Are you okay?' I felt her grasp my wrist.

I fell on my knees as they gave in.

'Are you okay?' she asked again. I was not *okay* at all. I felt scared but I knew what it was. It was not something new to me. Yet, it was as frightening as it was eight years ago—when it happened for the first time.

It was a seizure attack—something they call *fits* in general terms.

My left arm began to flail. And in no time, I was on all fours.

My vision was almost black now. I could feel Hari's strong arms around me. He might have rushed in watching me having fits. He was trying hard to hold me tight, but it was of no use. My hands and legs were shaking so furiously that it was not easy for anybody to hold me. My body was not in my control.

I passed out seconds later and have no memories of what happened next.

~

The seizure attacks were the dark side of my life, the side that I never preferred discussing with anyone, not even with the ones close to me.

I was ten when I suffered a major head injury during a family picnic to River Narmada. Though the injury was not fatal, it left me with post-traumatic seizures—fits that result from brain injury. Initially, when I was a child, their frequency was extremely high. But as I grew, they became rare.

~

I had considered the proposal to be fucked. But I was wrong. A beautiful surprise waited for me after the school hours. As I dragged my feet to the school bus, utterly disappointed with the untimely fits that had ruined one of the most important moments of my life, I found Tara standing near the school bus door.

She had let her hair loose and now those beautiful curls dangled across her shoulders. Her lips were shining with rosy shade and her eyes seemed seductively dark. *Has she applied makeup again?*—I wondered.

'How are you now?' she asked, tenderly.

'I . . . I am . . .' I opened my mouth twice, trying to speak, but both the times my voice failed me. She had the power to turn me speechless just with a bat of her eyelashes. She could set my nerves on rush by just a touch. She could make me do anything and everything—by just saying a word. She owned me. And all I wanted was to be owned by her.

'I love you too.' She surprised me.

A joyous wave spread over me and I grabbed her hand. She did not pull it back this time. I led her to the back of the school bus and hugged her. The moment our bodies touched; a rush of warmth spread across me. I could feel a sensation in my heart and spine that I had never felt before. As my body covered in goosebumps, I felt her reluctance converting into acceptance, and slowly, she wrapped her arms around me. 'I love you,' I whispered in her curls.

'I love you too,' she repeated. 'Were you serious? Are you going to Mumbai?' she asked, pulling herself back.

'After the exams,' I said. 'But only for a few years. Once I get into Navy—we will get married.'

Tara laughed. 'And what if you fall in love with someone else in Mumbai?' she asked.

'Why will I fall in love with someone else when I'm in love with you?' I replied.

'But what if you do?'

'Not in this lifetime.' I hugged her again.

'Kunal Marathe,' I heard the Vice Principal's high-pitched thunder. We broke the hug with a sudden jerk. 'What the hell is happening here?' yelled the Vice Principal, throwing a deadly look at us.

Shit! We were caught.

Ideally, I should have been frightened, but I could not rub off the smile from my face. I was happy for I had got the love of my life—but the Vice Principal was not.

Anyway. That is how you get suspended from school for a week.

CHAPTER 2

Schooldays were over and I had moved to Mumbai.

'This is the best college for Merchant Navy in the city. Don't settle for anything less,' my 30-something cousin said. He handed me a brochure of *The Harbour Maritime Academy* as he sat next to the electric barbecue grill that he had set in the gallery of his newly purchased apartment on the ninth floor of one of the tallest buildings in Hiranandani Gardens, Powai. It was an affluent area in Mumbai. And it was to be my new *temporary* home.

As I checked the apartment, I became more impressed with every passing second. Starting from the elegant hardwood flooring to the chandelier that hung beautifully in the living room, everything screamed money. Even the view of the Hiranandani Gardens from the gallery was simply kickass.

I took a quick tour of the apartment and came up with only one word for it—luxurious. I wished I could be that rich.

Vikram—tall, dark, handsome, and rich—was a Merchant Navy Officer and my maternal cousin. He was the one who had suggested me Merchant Navy as a career option and promised to be my mentor and constant support.

Lucky for me, his vacation was coming to an end soon, post which, he and his wife were to set sail for a minimum of six months. That meant I had his lavish apartment to live in till the time I get admission in a decent college. Being a Compulsory Residential course, I was supposed to move to the college hostel once the session began.

'What's your poison—scotch, vodka, beer?' Vikram *dada* asked, making a peg of scotch for himself. It was the first time someone from the family had asked me for a drink. A sudden feeling of being grown-up washed over me. It felt good.

'I don't drink,' I replied honestly, rejecting his offer. And I was not lying. It was not the first time I had the opportunity to drink. My friends from school drank often and many times forced me to try as well, but I never caved.

'You can be frank with me. I am your cousin—not dad. Tell me what you drink,' he said, gesturing towards a mini bar stocked with a variety of alcohol.

'Seriously, *dada*, I don't drink,' I assured him flipping a piece of chicken breast on the grill.

'That's good . . .' He seemed impressed. His focus was on the grill as he placed marinated pieces of fish next to the chicken breasts. My mouth watered at the delicious smell of the chicken. 'You got to study hard, Kunal.' He glared at me to emphasize. 'Your parents have struggled a lot all through their lives. They have sacrificed a lot for your education. Don't let them down.' He finished in a grim tone raising goosebumps all over my body. I knew how much my parents had sacrificed for me, and now, it was my turn to do something good for them.

I nodded, taking a bite of the grilled chicken we had just prepared. It was yummy. Chicken was something I loved more than sex—or perhaps not. Well, truth be told, I could not claim it then as I was still lacking experience in the latter.

'My senior's son is also preparing for Merchant Navy. He is of your age,' Vikram *dada* spoke again as he helped himself with another peg. 'His name is Mahesh. I will introduce him to you. He is a sincere fellow. You can learn a lot from him.'

~

'You know why I want to join Merchant Navy? Because I want to travel the world and sleep with women of every ethnicity around the globe,' the so-called sincere fellow, Mahesh Ranawat, declared as he took an expensive-looking bottle of vodka out from Vikram *dada*'s mini bar.

I laughed.

Almost a month had passed since I had shifted to the beautiful city of Mumbai, and Vikram *dada*—along with his wife—had left for Hong Kong to join a cargo ship as the Chief Officer. He held up to his promise and introduced me to Mahesh almost three weeks ago. Though we were poles apart, we became good friends in a short span of time.

Mahesh was a strange character. Really strange! He usually had a cigarette in his mouth and an alcohol bottle in hand. He left no occasion to abuse or throw a punch at anyone who pissed him off. And to top it all, he never ever missed a chance to hit on any woman—literally any woman!

He was ridiculously spoiled but carried a strange charm. You could hate him at times, but you would still want to be around him.

And yes, he was carefree as fuck.

'Don't drink too much. What will Vikram *dada* think when he comes back and finds his mini bar empty?' I said sipping my coffee.

'Just that his baby brother has finally crossed puberty and is now a grown-up man,' Mahesh laughed as he filled a glass with vodka. 'Seriously, lighten up and take a drink.'

'I have told you so many times—I do *not* drink,' a slight irritation laced my tone.

'One day you will. One day when you understand that you were living a lie. One day when you see your biggest dream shattering into pieces. That day, my friend, you will drink,' Mahesh professed and emptied his glass in one big sip—neat.

'Why do you drink? What dreams of yours have been shattered?' I asked. He ignored my question as he stared at his empty glass. 'Boys of your age just look for a chance to smoke and drink. Nothing else! It's all drama.' I snatched his empty glass, which he was still staring at.

'One man's pain is other man's drama,' Mahesh commented lighting a fresh cigarette.

Doorbell rang.

'No . . .' I muttered in an irritated tone as I peeped through the door viewer. It was Kamna, my beautiful but annoying neighbour. I rushed to the kitchen and requested Mahesh to answer the door and tell Kamna that I was not home.

He gave me a weird look as he walked to the door. His expression read—*you are hopeless.*

'Hi. Where's Kunal?' I heard Kamna's voice as I stood at the kitchen door. It was dramatically high-pitched.

'He is in kitchen. Wait. Let me call him.' Fuck! Mahesh was annoying at times—well, most of the times. One look at a hot girl and he forgot my instructions. 'Dude. Someone's here to meet you,' he yelled.

'Coming,' I yelled back and dragged my feet to the living room. *Damn Mahesh!*

Kamna Tiwari was young, hot and single. Dressed in white mini skirt and pink sleeveless top, she indeed looked attractive. Her parents had given her perfect name, Kamna—which means *desire*.

She was holding a big glass bowl covered with a ceramic plate. My eyes fell on her legs. Gosh! She was smoking hot. 'I prepared butter chicken today.' She blushed for some unknown reason and offered me the bowl.

'Thanks,' I replied with a plastic smile and took the bowl from her hands. Even if I wanted to avoid Kamna, butter chicken was something I could never avoid.

'How sweet of you!' Mahesh gave her a broad smile. He was definitely flirting, but Kamna did not pay any heed. 'Come in. Please.' He invited Kamna with a gentle tone and made way for her, pushing me aside.

'It's almost 11, dude. She must head back,' I said checking the time.

'Why? She has been so kind to bring us this delicious food. I am sure she would like to have it with us,' Mahesh replied raising his eyebrows. I knew what he meant. He meant—*I want to spend time with her, and if possible, the night too.*

'I am sure she has plenty of butter chicken back at home. And it's not safe for her to be out at this hour,' I gritted my teeth. I just wanted to stay away from Kamna but Mahesh was making it so damn difficult.

'But I want to eat with you guys,' Kamna argued, a little enraged, and she tried to get in. 'And don't worry about my safety. I live in the same society. It's very safe here.' She rolled her eyes seductively. It might have worked if I was not with Tara.

But—*I was with Tara.*

'It's late, Kamna,' I said and blocked her way. 'See you tomorrow.' I waved a goodbye. After a few awkward seconds, she left.

'Are you crazy?' Mahesh grabbed me by the collar as I closed the door. He definitely felt betrayed as I had taken away his chance to flirt.

Kamna lived in the building next to ours. She shared a good rapport with my sister-in-law. Before my cousin and sister-in-law left for Hong Kong, Kamna and I had crossed paths only a couple of times. We barely spoke, just greeted each other.

And four days ago, out of the blue, she proposed to me.

Surprised, I declined her proposal politely and told her about Tara. Yes, Kamna was irresistible, but I was already committed.

'What the fuck?' Mahesh yelled, throwing his arms in the air after I told him all about Kamna and her proposal, and the fact that I told her a point-blank *NO*. 'You rejected her proposal? Have you even checked her ass?'

'I have a girlfriend, dude. And she is there in my city waiting for me. How can I cheat on her?'

'What an idiot!'

'Okay. I am an idiot. Fine,' I said in a high-pitched voice.

'You tell me—what would have you done if you had a girl who loved you, and you loved her too—and then, some other girl would have proposed to you? Tell me. What would have you done?'

'Me?' Mahesh placed a fresh cigarette between his lips. Lighting it, he took a deep drag and bent towards me. 'I would have fucked both.'

CHAPTER 3

'Long distance relationships never work,' Mahesh announced. His sincere tone made me pay attention. I thought he would give me some good advice, but he added, 'because you don't get to fuck every day. How can a relationship work like that?'

It was my mistake to keep wrong expectations from the wrong person on the wrong topic.

Although he was talking rubbish, there was some truth in his words. Long distance relations are challenging. They are not easy—never easy. In fact, if the peace of mind is a priority and you are an insecure asshole, it is better to quit on them. The only people who can hold on to the long distance relationships are those who are madly and deeply in love with each other, like Tara and I were—*or so I thought.*

~

Unlike today, staying in touch was not an easy task back then. There was no WhatsApp, the Internet was super-expensive and needed a laptop or PC to be accessed, and majority of students did not have mobile phones.

Luckily, I had a mobile—a second-hand black and white *Nokia 1100*—because I was away from home. But Tara did not. I so wanted to talk to her, listen to her voice every day, all day—but it was not possible.

The melody of her soulful voice was my lifeline, but I understood that talking to me over phone everyday was not easy for her. Her parents were extremely strict, kind of orthodox too. They even hated it if she had close friendships with boys—forget about having a boyfriend.

Tara still managed to call me once or twice a week, whenever she could, but it was difficult to evade her parents' prying eyes. She had once told me that her mother even kept track of every call she made and always hovered around her whenever she was on phone.

Bottom line—I tried to be an understanding boyfriend and never forced Tara to call me often.

~

My phone rang at around 2 a.m. I was fast asleep. Opening my eyes, I checked the phone. An unknown number flashed on screen. 'Yes . . . who's this?' I said, irritated. I had fallen asleep just a while ago.

'It's me . . .' My irritation transformed into excitement in a nanosecond as I heard the voice from the other end of the phone. It was Tara.

'I can't believe you called at night,' I said, smiling.

'I was missing you,' she said.

'I love you so much, Tara. Thanks for calling.' I kissed the phone.

'Love you too,' she laughed, probably realizing that I had kissed the phone. 'Guess what? I got a mobile. Dad gifted it to me today.'

'Wow! So now I can call you at any time?' I said as my joys knew no bounds. Being able to talk to Tara whenever my heart desired was my dream.

'No . . .' she said. 'I will give you a miss call whenever mom-dad are not around—call me only then. You know *na*—how they are?' She broke my excitement.

Damn her parents!

'By the way,' she continued, 'I have one more good news. I got admission in a reputed Engineering college.'

'Wow! Which college?' I asked curiously and she narrated about her college in detail. She chirped so happily that it made me jealous. For a flash of a moment, I cursed my decision of shifting to Mumbai for Merchant Navy. If I had not left Indore, I would have been with her in the same college.

It was almost 3 a.m. when she asked, 'What about your admission?'

'Tests and interviews are done. I am waiting for the results,' I said, still lamenting the fact that I was not with her.

'You will make it—I am sure.' Her confidence brought a smile on my face and gave me a moral boost. 'I will hang up now; it's too late. And Dolly is sleeping next to me.' Dolly was her younger sister—and also she kept a close watch on Tara on behalf of her parents.

'Tara . . .' I uttered her name.

I knew it was late, but I did not want to hang up. It was after days that we talked for so long.

'Yes . . .' I could hear her nervous smile. I guess she understood my desperation.

'We have been in relationship for so many months, and you still did not let me kiss you?'

'Did you ever try to kiss me?' she asked in a playful tone.

Fuck! I never did. I actually never tried to kiss her. What an idiot I was! I mean—really!

'This time when we meet, I am going to kiss you,' my deeply seductive voice must have given away my thoughts as she laughed. They were not simple kiss thoughts; my mind was soon full of all the 18+ stuff.

'We will see,' she said, mischievously.

'What—we will see? You said I should have tried to kiss you.'

'I just asked you—did you try to kiss me. I did not say you should,' she was teasing me now. A blushing smile escaped my lips. 'Alright now. Bye.'

'Tara . . .'

'Yes, Kunal.'

'I love you so much.'

'I love you too, sweetheart. Good night now. See me in your dreams.'

'I am going to kiss you in my dreams.'

She chuckled and disconnected.

That night, her unexpected call made my heart blossom. That happiness still soothes me. It was satisfaction that I never got even after spending several nights with a long list of women in the later part of my life—the part in which sex was in abundance, but love had died.

CHAPTER 4

The wait was over. The Gods were kind as Mahesh and I got admission in The Harbour Maritime Academy. It was the one that Vikram *dada* had recommended, the best college for Merchant Navy studies in Mumbai.

Soon, Mahesh and I moved into the college hostel. It was mandatory. Even in the hostel, we were roommates. We made sure that we stayed together.

Life seemed perfect now. I knew I wanted nothing more from life. I had a bright career ahead. My parents were happy with how things were taking shape and they were incredibly proud. To top it all, I had the love of my life—Tara—with me. What else could one ask for?

At that time, however, I had no idea all that happiness and all those dreams were about to shatter. I had no idea that it was the end of my perfectly fine, sober life and the beginning of an era that was full of filth and madness.

CHAPTER 5

Initially, despite our distance, Tara and I were closer than any other couple I knew—we were as thick as thieves. We shared minute details of our life over the phone—our new friends, our routine, our syllabus—we talked about anything and everything. We had not seen each other for months but we were always in touch. Thanks to her new mobile phone—we talked for hours every day. She used to speak more, and I simply loved to listen to her. Her words held an unspoken innocence and I found peace in them.

But, within the next few weeks—everything changed.

Hardly a month after her college life had begun, she started changing.

I did not see it then but that was the beginning of the end. Our small, full-of-love world began to fall apart. The soft-spoken, childish, and emotional Tara started vanishing. And she grew distant and aloof with each call.

A couple of weeks more and I felt she had lost interest in me as well as in our relationship. Her caring and inquisitive nature had disappeared. She no longer bothered about what was going on in my life—unlike earlier. Those moments when we both talked and laughed, discussed random things about our life over the phone seemed like ancient history.

A time came when I felt like she was calling me out of a sense of responsibility, not love. It seemed like she was being forced to do so and she hated me for it. She even started ignoring me and putting up excuses like she was in the library or her phone's battery was dying.

Some more days passed and she abruptly stopped talking to me. Whenever I called her, she would reject my call and would not even bother calling me back or leaving me a message. A week passed by, but she neither replied to my calls nor called me back.

It was driving me mad; doubts were clouding my trust and I was getting utterly frustrated.

One night I called her at around 1 a.m.—and that was when I got a huge blow. Her number was busy. And even if you are the most broadminded asshole ever born on this planet—you know what it means when your girl has no time to talk to you for days, and then, you find her number busy at 1 a.m.

I took a deep breath and called her again. This time, her phone was switched off.

'What the fuck!' I muttered, both confused and scared. *Did I imagine her phone busy?* Had it not been for her weird behaviour lately, I would have dismissed it as a nightmare.

'All okay?' Mahesh asked. He looked at my fucked-up face and sensed that something was wrong. 'What happened, dude? You look like a whore who has been fucked but not paid,' he laughed. That was indeed a nice piece of dialogue—worth mentioning—but at that time, all it did was to piss me off even more.

I glared at him angrily.

'Sorry,' he said raising his arms. He might have understood the gravity of the situation and backed off with his sarcasm. 'Tell me what's wrong?' he spoke again, now with a deep concern.

'I got to go to Indore.' My heart grew heavier with every passing second.

'No way, dude. We have exams from day after.'

'Fuck exams,' I said.

~

I landed at Devi Ahilya Bai Holkar Airport in Indore at around 8 the next morning. It was my first air trip. Coming from a middle-class family, taking a flight was a big deal for me—and that flight ticket sucked up my entire budget for the month. Yet, it did not bother me. Money was not on my mind, all I wanted was to meet Tara and sort out the doubts that were eating me up from within—ASAP.

I was trying to convince myself that all my doubts were just doubts—but finding her number busy so late at night had made me lose my peace of mind.

I wanted to inform Tara about my arrival, but her phone was still off. I had sent her an SMS before leaving Mumbai Airport though: *Coming to Indore. Will meet you in your college. Love you.*

'If you trust her, then why did you bring your ass running back to Indore?' Hari asked as I narrated to him the entire incident. His words made me realize that I had said 'I trust her' at least a dozen times during our conversation.

Hari was one of the few people in my life who had never disappointed me. He was on his way to an early morning movie show with his girlfriend, but when I called him and informed him about my arrival, he cancelled his plans and rushed to the airport to pick me up.

'Umm . . . well . . . just as a precaution,' I said. I literally had no words to answer him. I definitely trusted Tara but I could not get over that miserable feeling that was burning me up from inside.

'You are in Mumbai, dude. Forget Tara. Find someone better there,' Hari said while we were speeding across the city to JSVITS—Tara's college.

'Jo gyaan manga nahin woh chod mat,' I hissed and tried calling Tara again, the fourteenth time. It was still switched off. *What's going on?*—I wondered.

As we drove in Hari's Tata Indica, I could see that Indore was changing—a lot and very quickly. There were new buildings, malls and colleges being built almost everywhere. The city was developing—but I was not too pleased to see that kind of development. The charm and serenity Indore once held was sort of vanishing. Most of the soothing roads that were earlier surrounded by tall, green trees were being widened now, and the trees were disappearing.

I was so engrossed watching my beloved hometown that I did not realize when we had covered the distance of twenty odd kilometres until Hari parked his car in front of the giant iron gates of JSVITS. Indore had this fashion of huge, expensive school and college buildings that gave the impression of gigantic castles in the first look. JSVITS was no less.

'Before we get in, you got to keep one thing in mind,' Hari said as soon as we stepped out of the car.

'What?' I said as I scanned the area eagerly, looking for Tara.

'Things have changed, Kunal. Tara is now in college—not school. People change in college,' his cautious tone took me by surprise. It was hard to understand. Before I could ask him what he meant, I heard a cheerful feminine voice calling out my name—sadly, not of Tara.

I turned and saw Pragya, our school friend. She was running towards us. In some other scenario, I would have greeted and hugged her, but that day what crossed my mind was—*Great. A familiar face. Maybe she can take me to Tara.*

'Hey . . . you too study here?' Hari asked her.

'Yes,' Pragya beamed. 'How are you?' she asked me. She seemed genuinely happy to see old friends. But I was not, I had too much on my mind.

'Where's Tara?' I asked, completely ignoring her question. It was rude. I know.

'She did not come today,' Pragya said.

'Any idea—why?' I asked.

'She is very tensed these days, yaar,' Pragya said sympathetically. 'Poor girl.'

'What happened to her?' I asked, now worried for her well-being.

'Nothing much. Boyfriend issues,' Pragya said playing with her hair. I thought she was teasing me.

'There are no issues with me. In fact, it is Tara who is acting weird these days,' I said.

'Sorry?' Pragya's unusual tone scared me. 'I was not talking about you. I meant, her current boyfriend—Ronit.' Her words shook me to the core.

I stood frozen. Shocked. Confused. Enraged. Fucked. I stood like a lifeless body whose head has been decapitated seconds ago. I did not know how to react. I could find no good words to speak. And even if some words crossed my mind, I could barely bring them out.

'Let's go.' Hari grabbed my hand and pulled me towards his car. 'Let's sit somewhere and talk.'

I looked at Pragya—who by now seemed to have understood what had actually happened. A tear falling down my eye must have told her all. Her hands covered her mouth, which was wide-open in shock.

'Are you guys still together? I mean . . .' She paused, perhaps for a reply. I had no reply. She continued, 'Tara told me a few days ago that you guys broke up, and now she is dating Ronit.'

Those words crushed me to my bones. I just stared—not at her, but through her, into blank space, as if she did not matter, Hari did not matter, my life did not matter. Everything began to look like a lie—a big fucking lie.

'That's enough, Pragya,' Hari shouted and grabbed my hand again. His touch brought me back to senses.

'You knew it?' I asked Hari as I shrugged him off. I was breathing heavily.

'That makes no difference,' he said. 'It was too late when I came to know about it.'

I said nothing. I was being slaughtered from within. It was a feeling I can never express in words, no matter how hard I try. I felt fucked and broken. My love was fucked. My trust was broken. I was feeling as if I had lost it all.

'Kunal . . .' Hari spoke again. 'You have to move on, my friend.'

I still wonder what got into me that moment. I did

something I had never done before, ever. I grabbed Hari by his neck and pushed him hard against his car. I was so angry, I would have murdered anyone then and there—no matter who.

'You knew it. And you did nothing,' I yelled, enraged with betrayal.

'What could have I done?' he raised his voice but did not hit me back, which he could have done, but he did not. He was a true friend.

'You could have told me . . . at least.' I shook him hard. My hands were shaking now, and I felt my feet tremble. I punched his car—hard.

'Do you know when I came to know that she is cheating on you?' He paused a little trying to take a breath, my hand was still at his throat. 'I knew Ronit for a long time. He was a friend of mine. One evening, he told me that he is dating someone, and he also told me that he went to a friend's flat with that girl . . . and they . . . they did it there.' He paused again. 'Later, I came to know—that girl was your Tara.'

I could not believe his words initially. But as they sank in, my whole world shattered. If my hands were shaking before, they went numb now. Those words were too brutal for me to bear.

In that particular moment I understood why some people commit suicide after they are cheated in love. Because the thought of the person you love and trust more than yourself sleeping with someone else is too filthy to imagine.

They did it there—the words echoed in my mind again and again. I could feel my blood pressure shooting up. I could feel my heartbeat increasing. A strange feeling had occupied my mind. I was going mad. Perhaps, I had already gone mad.

CHAPTER 6

'*Chutiyaape ki bhi ek hadh hoti hai, bhosadike,*' Hari was barking at me. 'What the fuck is wrong with you? She cheated on you, she slept with another man—just forget her now.'

We were at McDonald's—waiting for Tara.

After crying like a kid for two days, skipping all my meals and spending sleepless nights, I had finally decided to meet Tara. Yes. She had cheated on me—but I still loved her. And I still wanted her.

Love. It kills your sense of judgement and makes you do utterly stupid things. I was ready to forget everything that had happened and start over again.

'She is hardly seventeen, too young to discriminate between good and bad,' I defended Tara.

'And how old are you, sir—sixty?' Hari said in a sarcastic tone.

'You won't understand.'

'Really?' he spoke again. 'She had sex with another guy. Sex! That too when she was still in relationship with you. Even a ten-year-old can say—it was wrong. And if she can have sex at seventeen, she can also understand that she is cheating on you. Are you mentally challenged? *Duniya ko chutiya bana lo, mere bhai, lekin kabhi apne aap ko chutiya mat banao.*'

Before I could think of some good philosophical words

to convince Hari—and convincing him was important—my eyes fell on Tara as she walked in through the glass doors.

I was surprised to see her. The chubbiness I loved was gone, her beautiful curls were impeccably straight, and she was not wearing the nose pin I was crazy about. She had changed drastically—just like Indore.

'Hey Kunal,' she said and took a seat. She was accompanied by another girl whom I did not notice earlier. The way Tara met me was painfully formal. I had at least expected a hug.

'Hi . . .' I replied softly, masking my emotions with a fake smile. I did not wish to give her any hints regarding my knowledge of her affair. I did not want her to feel guilty of her own deeds.

Tara quickly introduced us to her new friend whose name I forgot immediately. Few awkward seconds later, Hari and that girl walked out, giving me and Tara some privacy. Now we sat alone, sharing a strange smile. I knew what I wanted to say, but I did not know how to start. 'Why was your phone off?' I somehow started.

'I am happy that you came to Indore.' She ignored my question.

'Are you?' I felt a wave of relief pass through me.

She did not reply.

'Your friend—Ronit—he is spreading nonsense about you,' I said anxiously, thinking of better words. 'You are innocent, Tara—but the world is not. You should not be friends with such people.' I waited for her reaction, but she maintained her silence. The quiet made me restless and the next words came out as an impulse reaction. 'I am moving back to Indore. I will take admission in your college. I can't stay away from you.'

'No. You can't come back,' she shouted. I was bewildered with those words. I guess she realized that she had been too loud—and too blunt—and she lowered her pitch. 'I mean, what about Merchant Navy? It is your dream.'

'You are my dream, Tara.' I held her hand. She sat stone faced. My touch did nothing to her. 'I realized going away from you was the biggest mistake I ever made. We were so happy together. I should not have gone away.' Fuck! Tears trickled down my face.

I immediately wiped my face with bare hands and tried to smile. 'We will be together, Tara—forever. I am never going to go away after this. I will do Engineering from your college. I will be with you . . . because nothing . . .' I paused as another stream of tears poured out of my eyes. 'Because nothing is more important than you.'

I did not realize when those silent tears changed into heavy sobs. 'It was my mistake, Tara. A big mistake,' I cried. 'I love you and I can't live without you. I just . . . can't.'

I began wailing like a little child and that was the end of it.

A few days later, Hari told me that he never imagined that I could cry like that. I—from the days of school—had a manly image. I was opposite to what the boys would call cute. But that day, sitting in front of Tara, I cried like a teenage girl.

Hari told me that even the cruellest stone-hearted woman in the world would have melted seeing a man crying for her like that. But Tara . . . she did not.

'I am sorry, Kunal. We can't be together anymore. I am happy that you came to Indore because I wanted to tell you the truth. I realized it now that I never loved you. You were my infatuation—and now it is over for me,' was her reply—hard, brutal and flat.

KAMNA

CHAPTER 7

'What do you think went wrong?' I wondered aloud. It was the question that was burning me deep inside. 'Why did she ditch me?' I muttered, trying to light a cigarette, the very first time in my life. My eyes were moist, my hands were trembling, and my lips were trying hard to hold the damn cigarette that I was unable to light.

It was around 3 in the morning. Mahesh and I sat on the thick boundary wall built with huge chunks of stones some thirty feet above the howling waves of the sea—in Mumbai. The giant Gateway of India stood tall to our left, the historic Taj Mahal Palace Hotel on our back, and the dark endless Arabian Sea right in front of our eyes.

After meeting Tara, I could not find enough strength to go back home and bid farewell to my family. I did not want them to see me like that—broken and full of tears. The same evening, I took a bus back to Mumbai.

I loved Indore. Having my family, my friends, and my love—all in the same city, I had begun to see the place as a paradise. The city had given me everything that one could ask for. But it had begun to haunt me now.

'Don't light it—please.' Mahesh snatched the cigarette from my lips. I was rather expecting him to light it for me and force the smoke down my throat, but he surprised me.

'Look who's talking,' I said.

'Because I know what it is,' he said. A deep concern reflected in his tone. 'Once you develop a habit for this deadly smoke—it will be very tough to give it up. It will suck the life out of you. It will just make the things worse.'

'Worse than this?' I gave a humourless laugh that made his face turn morose. Snatching the cigarette back, I successfully lit it in the third attempt. Slowly, I took my first drag, deep down the lungs—and I coughed my ass off immediately.

It was horrible.

'Stop it,' Mahesh roared. He took the burning cigarette from my hand—I was still coughing—and threw it away. I saw the cigarette take a deep arc and plunge into the sea. 'I understand what you are going through. I know it is not easy. You loved her—but it is over now. You must move on. You have to forget her,' he insisted on each word.

'Forget her? It is love—not some bloody computer file that can be deleted with a click,' I said. 'I wonder how she could forget me so soon.'

'She made it clear to you, right? She never loved you. It was just an infatuation for her. And it is common at this age—not a big deal,' his tone was so casual that I felt an urge to push him down the wall, into the sea.

I took a deep breath to calm myself down, deep enough to suppress the urge to push him. 'If it was just infatuation, she should not have committed to me. She said she wanted to be with me forever. She said it many times.' I took another cigarette out of the packet of Marlboro Hard and lit it. This time, I took a slow and cautious drag, slowly inhaling the smoke, closing my eyes. That was my first successful puff.

I still regret it.

It filled my mouth with a disgusting taste. But it

somehow made me feel good. I wondered—*Why!* It gave me a deep satisfaction, as if that harshly bitter taste were worth.

The way Tara had cheated on me had disturbed me to the core. It was not just about our breakup—there was something more to it. She had not just broken my heart; she had killed my ability to trust anyone again. She made me feel like my life was nothing but a big sham—a massive lie. I considered her an innocent, emotional little girl. But she turned out to be the opposite.

I had begun to see myself as an idiot—a loser. It was the first time in my life that I felt that guys like Mahesh and many other friends of mine who changed partners like their clothes were better. And I was a fool.

My philosophy of life—and love—was undergoing major changes.

'You know what? Only a woman can heal the wounds given by a woman,' Mahesh suggested after a long pause.

'What does that mean?'

'It means—move on. Get a girlfriend. And don't think about that life-long love crap again. Just get into something casual. You know what I mean, right?' Had Mahesh said that a few days ago, I would have avoided it considering he was bullshitting again. But after the Tara episode, I felt like he was talking sense.

To be honest, the fact that Tara went to a flat with some guy and they had sex there—while we were still in a relationship—was making me more restless than the fact that she had left me. Every time I imagined it, my blood pressure shot up, my heartbeat increased, and I was filled with disgust.

'I am feeling sick,' I choked. The cigarette slipped through my fingers. I looked down the sea and grabbed my head. 'Fuck! I don't know what to do. Why did she do this to me?'

'Enough. That's enough,' Mahesh roared. Although his voice was muffled by the waves, it was loud enough to turn a few heads towards us. We were not alone there. In a city like Mumbai, you are never alone anywhere. 'You are acting as if your world has ended. You are not the only person in this world who has had a breakup. Stop this bullshit now.'

No matter how betrayed I felt, he was right. Breaking up with partner or being cheated in love is not something very uncommon. Almost everyone faces it. But then, everyone is a different person. Everyone has a different version of love. For me, love was something that would only happen once in the lifetime—back then.

'Why the hell are you shouting at me?' I cried. 'It was not my fault. I loved her. I trusted her. And I was honest in the relationship. She is the one who cheated—not me.'

Mahesh was silent. He was perhaps done with me.

I too remained silent for the next few minutes. And then, I looked down. My eyes were fixed at the strong waves of the sea hitting the stone wall below us. They seemed compelling. My ears concentrated on the thunderous noise they made over and over. My senses lost somewhere.

The howling waves seemed rather welcoming and peaceful. I closed my eyes, and without any further thoughts—I jumped.

~

'Woke up, idiot?' I heard Mahesh's voice the moment I

stirred. His words forced my eyes open. I felt terribly numb and weak. There was a heaving pressure on my chest, and I felt tied up. The first thing that caught my eyes was an IV inserted into my arm.

I was in bed at the Hiranandani flat in Powai. *How did I come here?* I gradually remembered what I had done. Damn it! I must have almost drowned. Last night's happenings flashed before my eyes.

Seconds after I took that foolish jump, Mahesh jumped into the sea—to save me. He knew I was a horrible swimmer and there was no way I could have swum back to shore in that tide. Some fishermen playing cards in their boats jumped along. The strong waves were enveloping me rapidly, but it took the fishermen and Mahesh five odd minutes to pull me out of the water.

That is all remembered. I had fainted after that.

My eyes then fell on Kamna. Dressed in a miniskirt and a sleeveless top—as always—she sat in a chair next to the bed. I closed my eyes immediately and pretended to be asleep again. 'What is this, Kunal? Are you this insane?' she scolded me in her same dramatic high-pitched voice. I opened my eyes and looked at her. 'That girl is not worth it. You cannot throw away your life for her.' Her voice held a deep concern for me—and I did not like it.

I turned to Mahesh, throwing a pissed-off look at him. Of course, he was the one who told her about Tara's betrayal. Who else could it be?

'Thank God, you are safe.' Kamna got closer and caressed my head lovingly. Her hands were soft and warm. Her eyes were filled with affection and care. I could see it.

How I wished it were Tara.

'I will get you some coffee. You will feel better,' Kamna spoke affectionately, placing her hand on my cheek. If it were Tara's, I would have held that hand and kissed it.

'I had no idea you are such a coward. That was insane. You simply jumped!' Mahesh yelled rubbing the burning end of his cigarette in a stainless-steel plate as soon as Kamna left the room.

'You are—' I started, but he cut me off.

'Suicide is for weak people, brother,' he said in a rather calm tone, but this time, I had to interrupt him, because he was under a wrong assumption.

'Excuse me . . . it was not a suicide attempt,' I clarified.

'Then mind explaining what the fuck was that?' he demanded pulling a fresh cigarette and lighting it. He looked so macho doing it; I wondered how I looked while taking my first drag.

'If I had to commit suicide, I would not have jumped in your presence.' I tried to get up but could not. I felt a strong pain in my back. Mahesh rushed to help me. 'Trust me, dude. I have no desire to die. And that jump was not a suicide attempt.' I was not lying. I was broken, I was lost, but I never thought of suicide as an option.

I was not that weak.

'Then why did you jump—to measure the depth of the fucking sea?' He definitely did not buy my story.

'I jumped because . . . because I felt like jumping,' I replied, honestly. I had no proper explanation for why I did something so stupid. I was depressed and the sea looked like an option to free myself from all my sorrow. I know it was stupid logic. I know it sounded senseless. But it was the truth. I had nothing else in my mind while jumping off.

'Your explanation is ridiculous,' Mahesh argued.

'So is love,' I replied.

'Alright. Cut the crap,' he said as Kamna walked back with a mug of hot coffee.

To be honest, her presence was making me uncomfortable. The way she looked at me was odd—it held sympathy for me. And I hated it. Or was it because I boasted so much about Tara in front of her and I was finally proven to be dumb. Or was it because I denied Kamna's proposal and she would now think—*Oh, so you chose her over me . . . serves you right, loser.*

Whatever! My own hypothesis irritated me further and I finally requested Kamna to leave—politely.

She looked at Mahesh helplessly, and then, back to me. 'Please . . .' I requested again, almost begged.

'Okay. Take care. And for God's sake please do not do anything stupid again,' she said spreading her hand over my forehead. She looked at me with those *poor-boy* expressions again and walked out. Before leaving, however, she turned to wave a goodbye and I saw tears shining in her eyes.

She undoubtedly loved me. And I wondered how I could not love her back.

This is what I hate about love—it is the most illogical phenomenon in the world. You fall in love with someone who ultimately treats you like a piece of shit. And then, you fail to develop feelings for the one who deserves them!

'That girl loves you,' Mahesh said after Kamna was gone.

'I know,' I heard sympathy for Kamna in my own voice.

'And still, you misbehaved with her?' He paused for a reply from me. I had no reply. He spoke again, 'Do you even know she is here since morning? She saw me with the taxi driver carrying you to the flat—and she panicked. I told her you were fine, but she did not take my word and called a doctor for you. She even skipped her classes—for you, dammit!'

'I will thank her.' I had no other words to say.

'I can't believe this.' Mahesh grabbed his head and walked to window. After gazing into the sky for around a minute, he spoke again, 'You should be with this girl.' There was an immediate raise in his pitch, 'Forget the *bitch* who cheated on you and accept the one who loves you.'

I did not like Mahesh calling Tara a *bitch*.

'Give Kamna a chance,' he stressed.

'I don't love Kamna,' I made myself clear.

'Then love her, idiot,' he yelled and walked to me. 'Isn't it love that you want?'

'I want Tara,' I said.

Mahesh mouthed *fuck* before turning away. I remembered seeing similar expressions on Hari's face when he tried to convince me to move on from Tara and I kept on repeating that I loved her. I realized I was disappointing a lot of close ones with my stupid behaviour. Well—I was disappointing my own self too.

'Mahesh . . . try to understand,' I said in a low, convincing voice. 'I am not able to forget Tara.'

'You are impossible.' Mahesh grabbed the mug of coffee that Kamna had left on the side table and offered it to me. 'Take this. You need it—along with some brains.'

'This is not what I need . . .' I gently pulled the needle of the IV out of my arm. It was excruciatingly painful. The puncture in my arm started to bleed. I pressed it hard to prevent it from bleeding further. Mahesh was looking at it in a disgusted way.

Leaving the bed, I walked—rather dragged myself—to Vikram *dada*'s mini bar in the drawing room. Mahesh followed me. Scanning through various bottles, I picked one up. RUSSIAN STANDARD VODKA.

'This is going too far,' Mahesh said.

'Were you not the one who said, "One day when you understand that you were living a lie. One day when you see your biggest dream shattering into pieces. That day you will drink." Cheers, bitch. The day has come,' I replied and opened the bottle.

That was my first proper drink—my entry into the world of alcohol.

And I don't regret it.

CHAPTER 8

There is something strange about alcohol and cigarettes. They kill you slowly and silently; they eat you up from within, piece by piece, moment by moment—you know it, you know they are killing you, yet you allow them to!

How strange!

That was the beginning of the dark phase of my life. I was rotting in the deep pits of hell. Worse, I was not aware that I was to fall further down. The worst was yet to come.

I was depressed and miserable. Each day of my life was confined to drinks, smoke, lazing around and thinking about Tara. Every now and then, Hari's gruesome words—*they did it there*—would pop up in my mind and I would make another peg just to forget those words.

I did not even realize when alcohol and cigarettes became an inseparable part of my life. They felt like a limb that I could never dare to cut off.

Strangely, I still wanted Tara back in my life. My love for her was not over yet. I wished every day—all day—that she would change her mind and come back to me.

Mahesh tried his best to help me overcome the grief. But he failed as much as I failed. Still, he proved himself to be a selfless friend who was there with me at every turn.

He was staying with me at Hiranandani, which meant he too was skipping the college. *Why should he suffer because of me?*—I cursed myself. And thus, I asked him to move back to hostel and resume college.

He tried to convince me to re-join the college and hostel with him, but I was in no condition to study. He even threatened to never go back to the hostel until I accompany him, but his threats did not persuade me.

After many sessions of discussions, promises, drama and even abuses, I convinced him to move back to the hostel. *'Mere lavde lage pade hain, yaar. Andar tak maa chud gai hai.* I need some time alone, brother. You leave. Join college. I will join you as soon as I am fine,' I said.

Mahesh finally left.

~

In those days, I realized the depths of Kamna's love for me. Every single day, she brought me food, without failing—twice. I ate it sometimes but threw it away mostly—I had lost my appetite. There were days when I did not even bother to open the door for her, yet she left the food with a loving note at my doorstep. I wondered how selfless she must have been to tolerate my insulting behaviour.

She loved me madly. And it was my misfortune that I failed to love her back—a guilt I will carry to the grave.

I tried to speak to Tara every single day—but failed. She had changed her number and did not share the new one with any of our common friends.

I often begged Hari to talk to her; he was reluctant because he hated Tara to his core now. '*Gelchode* . . . you are crying for her and she is fucking around with that bastard,' he yelled at me once.

'Please, Hari. I am dying to talk to her. Please request her to call me,' I pleaded.

He agreed.

'Don't you dare ask me to talk to that *bitch* again,' Hari told me on phone the next day. 'I told her that you are suffering for her . . . and . . .'

'And?' I asked.

'And she said—*usko bol drama bandh kar de ab.*'

~

I had gulped in a whole bottle of vodka that night. I was not just tipsy; I was crazy fucking drunk.

'I won't let you go,' I muttered and dialled Tara's landline number. Like all the previous attempts, the call was answered by her mother. The devil inside me wanted to ask her for Tara, but even in my drunken state I was not ready to do anything that would create a trouble for the girl I loved.

I then called Hari, and then, Mahesh. None of them received the call. It was around 2 a.m. They were definitely fast asleep. Then, I made a huge mistake—a blunder. I called Kamna.

'I can't believe you called at this time of night,' she said even before I could say *hello*. I recalled I had said something similar to Tara when she had called me the first time at night.

Memories hit me and I disconnected the call.

I felt bad. Not for me—but for Kamna. She loved me as madly as I loved Tara. And I did not love her—just like Tara did not love me.

Fuck love. It creates more broken hearts than happy couples.

Kamna called me back. 'Why did you disconnect the call?'

'Can you come to my place?'

'Now?' she sounded confused. 'It's not possible, Kunal. See the time. What would I tell my parents?'

'Don't tell them. Just sneak past them. They must be sleeping anyway,' I suggested, selfishly. I would have never given such a suggestion to Tara. I would have never wanted her to take any risk that could put her into trouble.

'Dad will kill me if he finds it out. Can I come in morning?'

'It's fine,' I said lighting a cigarette and disconnected the call.

My phone rang immediately. 'Are you fine?' I heard worry and anxiousness in Kamna's voice.

'Yes. I am fine,' I replied and disconnected again.

She called back. 'You don't sound fine. I'm coming.'

She loved me beyond limits, indeed.

The doorbell rang fifteen odd minutes later and I stumbled across the drawing room to answer it with a bottle of vodka in my hand.

I was a bit shocked to see Kamna standing in my doorway. I was so drunk that for a moment I had completely forgotten that I had invited her minutes ago.

She stood in front of me, dressed in black leggings and pink zip-up hoodie. I stared at her—from top to toe. It was the first time I looked at her that way. She looked more seductive than usual.

'Are you okay?' she asked, concerned. Her eyes said she wanted to come in, but her body language screamed otherwise. She looked confused—as confused as I was.

I abruptly grabbed her hand and pulled her in.

'What are you—' she whispered but I placed my finger on her lips. She gasped at my touch. I pushed the door close with my foot and pressed her against the wall. She was quiet, but her eyes did all the talking. They were asking me to move forward—or perhaps, so I thought.

I pushed myself onto her and covered her body with mine. She felt soft and fragile against my body and smelled of jasmine.

'You are drunk. You should not—' she was out of words as I placed a soft kiss on her neck.

I looked up and we stared into each other's eyes for a long moment silently. I felt her chest rise and fall heavily against mine. I moved my lips closer to hers and felt her shiver.

She closed her eyes.

Without kissing her lips, my lips reached her neck again. 'How much did you drink tonight?' she asked, motionless.

I paused for a moment but ignored her question. Wrapping myself against her, I began kissing her neck furiously. Her breathe was getting faster with every moment.

'You are drunk,' she spoke again.

I kept quiet and continued with kissing. She raised her hands to stop me, but I grasped them and held them behind her back. She did not resist.

I kissed her again, and then, moved down. My lips reached her cleavage and with one free hand I held the zipper of her hoodie to open it. I was losing myself, and the fact that she was not resisting was encouraging me to move further.

I pulled the zipper of her hoodie down and grabbed her by waist tight.

'Do you love me?' she asked out of the blue.

I did not reply. I did not want to reply.

Avoiding her question, I forced her to turn and pushed her into the wall hard. 'Kunal . . .' she yelped. I mistook it for pleasure. I pulled her hoodie off and threw it aside. She was wearing a thin tube-sleeved top underneath it. I hastily pulled it—and she finally resisted.

Pushing me, she turned to face me.

'Do you love me?' she asked again, this time a little louder, placing her palm on my chest. I tried to get closer again, but she pressed her hand hard.

'I asked you something—Do you love me?'

'Does that matter?' I hushed.

'Yes. It does matter. I am a decent girl—not some whore.' Her words felt like a slap to me and brought me back to the senses. In the blink of an eye, my drunken state faded, and I could clearly see through my actions.

'But you love me, right?' I asked, much sober now.

'I loved the guy who knew what true love is. I loved the guy who never looked at me the way you are looking at me today. I loved the guy for whom love was more important than the shit you are doing right now,' she said. 'And you—do not look like that guy anymore. You have turned into something pathetic . . . something disgusting.'

'But wasn't it *this* that you wanted?'

'I can get *this* anywhere. There are thousands of men out there who would be ready to fuck a girl if given a chance.'

Her words were fierce. I pulled myself together and took a step back. Yes, I was drunk. Yes, I was turned on. Yes, I wanted to get physical with her. But I was not a molester. I was not a monster.

I wondered how some men force themselves on women. But I was not one among those sick men.

As her words sunk in with me, I felt ashamed. She did not deserve that. Her words—though brutal—were right without a shred of doubt. I had become something disgusting.

I kept my silence. But she spoke again, 'I love you, Kunal. I love you beyond your imagination. But I don't want to be treated like this. I want love in return of love. If you ever think you can give me that love—I'm just a call away. I would love to make love with you—but that should be love, not the lust you are filled with at this moment.'

She waited for me to speak. But I had no words to speak.

Ultimately, she picked her hoodie up from the floor and left without another look at me.

I don't remember for how long I sat by the door with the bottle of Vodka in one hand and cigarette in another after she was gone. I was angry at myself.

How did I do this to her? She was the only girl who gave a fuck about me—and I screwed it all. When did I turn into this rotten piece of shit?

I was no longer the man I was proud to be. I was no more the man Kamna was proud to love.

'Fuck . . .' I screamed and hit the bottle against a wall and regretted immediately. It was the last bottle I had!

CHAPTER 9

I never loved Kamna, so I never called her back. What I did that night was something I regretted more than anything. I made mockery of the woman who actually loved me. My behaviour was sick. That was the last night I felt pity for myself, because after that night, my self-pity had turned into self-loathing—and it stayed that way for a long, long time.

Months passed, but I was still stuck there, in the valley of darkness where Tara had pushed me, in the depths of the valley of darkness where I had pushed myself further.

I left the plush Hiranandani flat and moved to a cheap, run-down room in old Mumbai, not too far from the Masjid Bunder Railway Station. It was an area surrounded by perfume sellers, mutton shops and restaurants specializing in kebabs. The mixed stench of strong perfumes and raw meat was unbearable. Still, I moved in, because it was the only option in my budget—which was almost negligible. It was the only room I came across during my hunt for a shelter where the owner was ready to rent out without a security deposit, which—in Mumbai—can be as high as ten times of the monthly rent.

Bilal, my property broker, had given me a brief background about my new home. It was a dance studio years ago; however, it had been shut after the owner eloped with his mistress, and his heartbroken wife—who was the dance teacher of the studio—committed suicide.

Wow—was how I reacted after learning that. 'The world is full of cheaters,' I added.

My room was on the first floor. And if the location of the building and the building itself was horrible, the room was even more pathetic. It was a large three hundred square feet room with cracked walls and broken glass windows that were decorated with pigeon poop. A huge beehive was stationed in a window adjacent to mine and a new one was under construction near it.

I was provided with nothing more than a ceiling fan that made more noise than cool air, a tube light that tried sporadically to light the room, a pathetic old metal bed that creaked with every movement, and a wooden wardrobe—with a cracked mirror—that looked like an antique.

The place was no less than hell if compared to the plush Hiranandani apartment.

What was I doing in Mumbai now? Well, nothing!

I had left college. It was not easy, but I managed to hide that fact from my parents. They would have gone mad if I had told them that. I had no job in hand, and no 'glorious career' ahead, and I was almost penniless. I lived off the money my father used to send for my college and hostel fees.

I had no mood to re-join the college or return to Indore. And thus, I was there, passing my days in a penurious corner of the City of Dreams—with no dreams.

~

One night at around 1 a.m., I found all my vodka bottles empty. After licking every drop out of them, I stepped out of the room to find a liquor shop. I was thirsty and wanted my elixir at any cost.

Stumbling across the street, I made my way to the rickshaw stand. It was cold that night—something rare in Mumbai. Focussing on the road, I was puffing on my cigarette non-stop. The streetlights were dim, and the road looked darker than usual. *What the fuck happened to the streetlights?*—I wondered.

It was too dark for me to see the ditches and potholes. Almost every dog I came across was barking at me. '*Aai jhavaade,*' I cursed and kept walking.

Before I could find a rickshaw, I found two cops blocking my way. They were from a group of cops standing near a police Jeep. They were looking at me comically, as if they had never seen a guy before.

'Are you drunk?' one of them asked me.

'And who are you to ask that—my mom?' I replied.

'Get in the Jeep,' the other cop yelled.

'Why. W-w-what have I done?' Suddenly, my knees gave in and it was difficult for me to stand. The cop held me up, making a disgusted face.

'*Patil Saheb . . .*' A huge, dark man came running to us from nowhere. I focussed my eyes to see his face in the dark. It was Bilal, the property broker who had helped me get the room. 'He is my friend, *Saheb,*' Bilal told the cops. 'I apologize on his behalf.'

'Apologize? Apologize for w-what?' I slurred. 'Do I look like a thief, a murderer—a rapist?'

'*Lekar jaa bewde ko,*' one of the cops told Bilal and they walked to their Jeep.

'What's wrong with you?' Bilal asked me.

'What's wrong with me? Bloody what's wrong with them? Is it a crime to drink in Mumbai?' I felt enraged.

'No, it's not. Unless you are walking on the streets without a shirt,' Bilal laughed.

'*Aai jhavali . . .!*' I looked down at my chest. Yes. I had no shirt on me!

'And why are you wearing goggles at this time of night?' he asked, confused. I now knew the reason behind the unusual darkness.

Alcohol. It makes you mad.

~

'So . . . rich guy exploring the poor area of the city, hmm?' Bilal asked, making two pegs of rum with his heavy hands. He was dressed in a white *kurta pajama*. Having a thick chain of gold hanging around his neck, his fingers were adorned with heavy gold rings. He looked more like a politician than a property broker.

We were at my room.

Thankfully, Bilal had a stock of liquor—to sell in black—at his place. He brought two bottles of rum—since he had no vodka—for the night.

'What makes you think I am rich—this fucked up room I live in?' I said sarcastically, lighting a cigarette.

He laughed.

'You hardly step out of the room. It means you are not working. And looking at this stock of empty vodka bottles, anyone can say your father must be a rich man to send you so much money,' he insisted scanning the room. His guess was not illogical, considering the entire room was littered with vodka bottles. Yet, he was wrong.

'Alcohol and cigarettes are the only things I spend money on. I hardly have any other expenses,' I told him. 'And by the way, my father is a middle-class truck owner, he drives the truck himself, and my mom is a government employee. They send me money for education—that I burn in this,' I finished, my tone filled with guilt, and I took a large sip from a bottle of rum.

'I see . . .' Bilal snatched the bottle from my hand and passed me the peg he had made. He glanced around the room, as if scanning it. 'But it is not a bad room,' he spoke again.

'Really?' I raised my eyebrows.

'Of course. Consider it this way—you have full freedom here. The owner has moved to Hyderabad and now there is no one to check on you. Do whatever you want. You can even bring your girlfriend here. Spend all night with her. No one will object.'

Thanks for spoiling my already fucked-up mood, asshole—I cursed Bilal in my mind and threw an angry look at him.

'No girlfriend?' he guessed. 'Even that is not a problem. I can arrange one for you—one night's girlfriend. You know what I mean, right?' he finished with a creepy smile.

'How much for the bottles?' I opened my wallet. 'Take the money, have a peg—and leave.'

'Why are you so angry?' Bilal took a sip. My words did not even bother him. 'Had a breakup or what?'

'It was not a breakup—it was a betrayal,' I said in low voice. Another sip.

'You drink so much because you are trying to forget someone?' he analysed my situation. For a change, he sounded sincere.

'I don't know.' I paused and took a puff. It was after a long time that I had an audience to listen to my pain. It took me around a minute to speak again, 'I am so lost, so fucked. You know what . . . never consider someone everything, because when that someone is gone—you are left with nothing.' One more sip. 'Were you ever cheated in love?'

'No,' Bilal said. 'But I did cheat someone who loved me. And I got punished for my crime.' Now his face seemed covered with grief. The alcohol was doing its magic on both of us.

'Care to explain?'

'Aafrin . . . her name was Aafrin. She was the most beautiful girl in my *chawl*. And I, like every other young boy, was attracted to her. After spending days trying to impress her, when I proposed to her, she said she was looking for a permanent relationship. She made it very clear to me that she wanted a man who would never leave her.'

'And you were that man?'

'No. I was not. But I lied to her that I was that man. I just wanted her as my girlfriend. To be honest, I just wanted to sleep with her. So, I made a fake promise—that I will marry her once I am settled.' He paused for a sip and spoke again. 'After being in a relationship for few months, and sleeping with her like a hundred times, I was bored of her—like any other man.'

'Not all men,' I interrupted.

'Well—most of the men,' Bilal said.

'Alright. What then?'

'Then I left her. Another girl caught my fancy.'

'Disgusting . . .'

'It's not over yet,' Bilal said, taking the burning cigarette from my hand. 'After I left her, she came to me crying—many times. She said she loved me. She said she trusted me. She said she wanted to marry me. But I—being the *disgusting* man I was—made it clear that I was no more interested in her.'

'People like you should be hanged till death.'

'Well, I was not hanged till death—of course,' Bilal said passing another weird smile. 'But I was indeed punished for my deeds.'

'How?'

'One evening, I was shocked to see policemen at my door. They had come to arrest me. Later, I came to know that Aafrin had made a complaint against me to the police.'

'And you were arrested? Arrested because you dumped your girlfriend?' I was shocked. I never knew such a law existed!

'As per Indian law, if you promise to marry a girl and have sex with her—you will have to marry her. If you refuse the marriage, it is a crime. It is considered rape!' he explained. 'So finally, I served three years in prison as a rapist.'

'Serves you right.'

'That was my story,' Bilal said with a humourless chuckle. 'Now tell me yours.'

'I . . .' I lit another cigarette and leaned back on the edge of my bed. 'I just want to forget everything and get out of the shit I am stuck in.'

Bilal smiled and made the next round of pegs for both of us. After a long silence and a couple of sips, he spoke, 'Ever heard of LSD?'

'No. What's that?'

He fished out his wallet from *pajama*. Given the way this man adorned himself with gold jewellery, he really did lack taste in wallets. It was a partially torn brown leather wallet. He focussed on my face for a moment, as if trying to read if I was ready, and then, he slowly pulled a small plastic pouch out and gave it to me. There were colourful tablets in the pouch, with Mickey Mouse, Donald Duck, Popeye, and other cartoon characters carved on them.

'You must be joking. What the fuck is this?' I scanned the tablets.

'It's the gateway to heaven—a motherfucking cure to every problem. Something that you need to get out of the shit.'

If this one tiny tablet can get me out of my misery, this is what I need—I thought. I was too drunk to think practically. Without wasting any time, I pulled one tablet out—it had Mickey Mouse engraved on it—and I swallowed it before Bilal could give any further instructions.

~

Tuck! Tuck! Tuck! I heard a knocking on door.

I was fast asleep until those knocks woke me up. I was too lethargic to leave the bed and my head throbbed with strong pain. I buried my head in pillow, hoping whoever it was on the door would just go away.

Knocks continued.

'So raha hoon, bhenchod,' I screamed at the door.

Tuck! Tuck! Tuck! Tuck! Tuck! Tuck! The knocks grew louder.

'Who the fuck is there?' I yelled. As soon as I opened my eyes and looked out of the window, sunrays hit my eyes. It felt like somebody had stabbed them. It took me a couple of minutes to finally leave the bed and look around. Bilal had already left. But when? I hardly remembered anything that happened after I took that magic pill.

I had a smile on my face when I thought about it—the tablet worked for I had slept peacefully without any horrifying nightmare after a long time.

Tuck! Tuck! Tuck! The idiot at the door—whoever the fuck it was—seemed too eager to see me. *'Thand pakad, bhosadike,'* I muttered and walked to the door. Shivers crawled up my spine the moment I opened the door. *No. It was not possible.*

Tara was standing in front of me. Yes. Tara.

How is it even possible?—I wondered. I was stunned in the moment, I just stood there staring at her, open-mouthed. She was there, right in front of my eyes. 'Tara,' I muttered and fell to my knees. 'How did you find me?'

'I am sorry, Kunal,' she said. 'I should have never broken up with you. I understood it now that no one can ever love me like you do.' I had dreamt of those words for long. I was dying to listen to them.

She gently caressed my head, and instinctively, I buried my face in her waist. Finally, my prayers had been answered. I stood up and took her in arms; I hugged her tight with no intention of ever letting her go. My eyes were moist. 'I love you,' I said and kissed her forehead gently.

'I love you too.' She wrapped her arms around me. It was the same way she had hugged me the day I had proposed to her in the school. 'I am sorry,' she said again.

'Shh . . . there is no need to say sorry.' I placed my finger on her lips and led her into the room. 'You are too young. It happens. Let us forget the past and start afresh.'

She sat on my bed and not leaving her hand I sat on the floor. Placing my head in her lap I spoke, 'I can't believe you are here.' Tears sparkling in my eyes. I was flooded with emotions—good ones. After a long time, I was happy, so damn happy. 'I am never going away from you again. We will be together—forever,' I said, kissing her palm.

'But you will have to,' she said.

'Sorry—what?' I looked up at her utterly confused, not sure what she meant.

'You will have to go out of the room—at least for a while,' she finished with a devious smile.

'Why?' I asked.

'Because Ronit is here,' she said, and I felt my heart stop with a sudden jolt. Before I could understand what the hell was going on, she continued, 'Ronit and I needed a room, so we came here—to your room. You anyway know about it. This is not the first time. Hari told you, didn't he? We went to a friend's room and *we did it there.*' She had a wicked smile on her face—like a witch. 'Come, Ronit. Let us not waste time,' she said, looking at the door.

I followed her gaze. To my shock and utter disbelief, Ronit—whom I had never seen before—was standing at the door.

'Let's make love, Ronit,' Tara said seductively, slowly unbuttoning her shirt.

Horrified and angry, I screamed, 'Ronit, *madarchod.*'

I was slapped—by Mahesh! Fuck! It was a dream—a nightmare—another nightmare! *'Bhosadike, pagal ho gaya hai kya?'* Mahesh yelled.

CHAPTER 10

'So, you started taking drugs?' Mahesh said, dead angry, as he arranged packets of Maggie and some other stuff on cooking platform. It had become his Sunday ritual. He would come by every Sunday to check on me and would also bring some essentials.

'I need to find a job. How long will you spend your pocket money on me?' My head was in my hands. I was still shocked with the nightmare.

'Don't try to change the topic. Why did you take that drug?'

'I was drunk. And I had no idea—it was a drug. Bilal just told me it was something called LSD,' I confessed.

'LSD is a fucking drug,' Mahesh shouted. 'If you ever do drugs again, I swear on my mom—I will throw you back to Indore.'

'I will not.' The word *Indore* gave me chills.

'I miss the person you were,' Mahesh spoke after a long pause, pouring some milk into two coffee mugs.

'So do I,' I whispered, lighting a cigarette.

'There is still time, Kunal. Stop this nonsense and come back to college,' he almost begged.

'Those books—thick as fuck—they need concentration and interest. And look at me . . . do I look interested in any of them anymore?'

'All this just because a girl dumped you?'

'No. All this because there is no fire left,' I gave the most honest answer possible. 'The day I really feel like doing something—I will. Trust me. It is just a bad phase. It will go away.'

'It will not go away until you decide to,' Mahesh said as he tore open a coffee pouch.

'Then I will decide it soon.'

'How soon?'

'Pretty soon . . .'

He did not argue further and began to put coffee powder in the mugs.

'Why coffee? Let's have some rum,' I said with a puff. 'We have not taken drinks together in a long time.'

'I don't drink anymore.' His words came to me as a shock.

'Fuck . . .!' The cigarette dropped out of my mouth. 'You're kidding, right?'

'I am serious. My girlfriend asked me to swear on her that I won't drink and smoke again. So, I gave that shit up.'

'You fucking with me?' My mouth hung open at his reply. *Mahesh in a serious relationship!* That was worth a drink. I opened the bottle of rum.

Women! They are strange. One good woman made that spoilt brat give up alcohol and cigarettes. And one wrong woman changed me from a sober person into an alcoholic. They are right when they say that women are more powerful than men. They can fuck the shit out of us.

'By the way, who is this new girlfriend of yours?' I asked.

'New chick?'

'It's not casual this time. I am committed to her.' Mahesh looked serious. That guy was changing for good. Actually, he was becoming me—in reverse.

'What happened to your plan of sleeping with women of every ethnicity around the globe?' I mocked.

He just smiled. 'I have changed now.'

'Good.' I took a big sip. 'What's her name?'

'That doesn't matter.'

'It does. I need to know the name of the girl who changed my friend so much. She must be someone very special, hmm?'

'I did not tell you about her for a long time,' Mahesh said. 'I was worried about how you would react. I thought, maybe, you will feel bad about it.'

'Why would I feel bad about it?' I was confused.

'Because her name is Kamna,' Mahesh said.

~

'When you left Hiranandani and moved here, Kamna called me often. She was worried for you,' Mahesh started, leaning over the cooking platform, holding a mug of hot coffee. I sat on my bed and listened to him silently, holding a peg of rum in my hand. 'She often cried over you, begged me to help you. She was so sweet, so sincere, so innocent. She was too good to not fall for. I did not even realize when I started loving her.'

He paused and waited for my reaction. I just nodded.

He was right, Kamna was too good to not fall for—

unless you are an idiot like I was.

'Then one day,' he continued, 'while she was asking about you, I told her, "I don't know if Kunal loves you or not—but I love you." And I meant it.'

He seemed torn with guilt, although he had done nothing wrong. It was Mahesh who had repeatedly asked me to pursue Kamna, but it was I—the stupidest asshole alive—who had ignored his suggestion. I remembered telling him to stop talking about Kamna whenever he started her topic.

'Come here,' I said and kept the glass of rum aside.

'I thought you will hate me for this—so I failed to gather the courage to tell you about us,' Mahesh confessed, walking to me. 'I hope you are not angry with me. I really love her. And if you would have loved her, I would have never let that thought cross my mind. You know—'

'Shh . . .' I got up and hugged him. 'Why would I be angry? You are my best friend, and your happiness makes me happy. She is a gem of a girl. Just make sure you never break her heart.'

'I will not,' Mahesh promised as he hugged me back.

Human nature is weird. I should have been happy for Mahesh—he finally had an amazing girl in his life who was setting everything right for him. I should have been happy for Kamna—she had finally fallen in love with someone who loved her. But—I was not happy. I felt fucked. I felt like another part of my life had been cut off that day. But—I did not let Mahesh have the slightest hint of the turmoil that was taking place within me.

Since both of those wonderful people in my life were now happy with each other, I too pretended to be happy.

What else could I do?

ALIA

CHAPTER 11

'Nanga soya ho toh fatafat uth aur kapde pehen,' Mahesh said from the other end of phone. It was his eighth call since morning—the only one that I answered. A yawn escaped my mouth as I opened my eyes. I was still in bed—almost naked as usual.

Mumbai was drenched in rain and half of the floor of my room was already covered with water. I had been planning to repair the broken windows—or at least shield them to block out the rain—for some time now, but all my plans drowned in vodka—just like my life.

I looked around, there was nothing valuable in the room that water could damage.

'Hello? You there?' It was Mahesh again. His repeated calls were pissing me off now.

'Wrong number,' I said and disconnected the call.

As a habit, I checked my phone before going back to sleep again.

Holy shit! There were thirty-two missed calls—seven were from home. *Did someone die?*—I wondered as I panicked for a second, but in the next moment, I could not bother more. *Fuck it.* I went back to sleep.

The phone buzzed as soon as I closed my eyes. It was Mahesh again.

I answered it as he had totally destroyed my sleep by now. Picking last night's vodka bottle up from the floor, I kept the phone by my right ear. 'I hope you are dressed,' Mahesh said.

'How the fuck it matters. I am neither a girl nor gay,' I said in harsh voice, gulping some vodka down. It was my way of wishing myself *Good Morning*.

'Happy birthday, asshole,' Mahesh wished me.

What kind of a person forgets his own goddamn birthday?—I asked myself.

Fine. It was my birthday—my nineteenth birthday to be precise. So that was the reason I had so many missed calls. After all, there were a few people left who gave a damn about me—even if I had stopped giving a damn about anyone and everyone.

'Thanks, brother,' I said into the phone and a short smile broke around my lips.

'I am standing outside—with Kamna. Open the door,' Mahesh said. And I was traumatized.

'Shit.' I jumped from the bed immediately. *Damn it!* I felt drained and energetic at the same time. There was no way I wanted Kamna to see me in that condition. I scanned the room again, earlier I thought that the rainwater had nothing to damage, but all of a sudden, I could see a lot of things that could do a lot of damage—to me. There were loads of vodka bottles and cigarette butts scattered all around the room.

'Give me five minutes. Don't you dare bring her in just yet. Stay there—please.' I disconnected the call and began with gathering all the vodka bottles that were spread around. Within seconds, I was holding a little too many of them and they started falling off my hands.

Having no place to dump, I ended up throwing them on the bed.

Dozens of bottles were gathered on the bed sheet in no time. 'They are not on the floor, at least,' I mumbled and stared at the huge pile.

'Now the cigarette butts.' I quickly found the broom that Mahesh had bought for me long ago. It was unused. Now that the vodka bottles were out of the way, I was able to find a lot of things I had misplaced overtime—like my long-lost underwear, my sunglasses, a packet of peanuts and what not. I ignored everything and decided to give a quick sweep to the floor. It took me a good amount of time to clean the floor, not because there was so much crap on it—which was of course the case—but because the rainwater made it too tough to sweep. Still, I did my best.

Mahesh called me twice in between, but I only said, 'wait', and disconnected both the times. He was definitely getting impatient. I heard a huge thud on the door, and it made me panic even more. 'Just a minute,' I yelled and collected all the cigarette butts on an old newspaper and threw that on the bed. I looked around again and after deciding that throwing away all those bottles and cigarette butts down from the window was not a good idea, I went for the last option—wrapping everything in bed sheet, I tossed it in the bathroom, sincerely hoping that Kamna would not ask to use the bathroom.

It took me another two minutes before I could finally put clothes on and was ready to face Kamna. Taking a deep breath, I opened the door. Ever since Mahesh had told me about his relationship with Kamna, I had been dreading this moment. I was too nervous to face her as I was ashamed of what I had done the last time I saw her.

As I opened the door, my eyes fell on her stunning face. She wore a nervous smile.

She had not changed a bit.

It was hard for me to look into her eyes. I was still filled with guilt. I somehow managed to throw a short smile at her. She smiled back.

'Happy birthday, brother.' Mahesh hugged me and patted my back.

'Many, many happy returns of the day,' Kamna wished me softly. She maintained her distance from me.

'Thanks,' I said and made way for them to enter.

Kamna scanned the ceiling as she quietly sat in the bed. I too looked up. It was filled with cobwebs. I wondered how I never noticed them—given that all I did all day was to lie in that godforsaken bed and stare at that godforsaken ceiling.

Mahesh was still standing, perhaps wondering where had all those empty vodka bottles and cigarette butts disappeared. I made myself comfortable on a dry patch of the floor, resting my back against wall.

'You have lost a lot of weight,' Kamna said.

'Hmm . . .' I was wondering how to react.

'This is for you.' Mahesh threw a fabric travel garment bag—having a blazer in it—and two shopping bags on the bed. Usually, I would not have gotten up and bothered to check, but Kamna looked excited, and I did not wish to disappoint her.

'I don't need this,' I said, scanning through the bags. It had clothes.

'Vodka and cigarettes are not the only things you need.' Mahesh walked to the bathroom. Before I could stop him, he opened the bathroom door and his eyes widened. He threw *you-are-impossible* look at me and walked back to the bed. 'We arranged a small party for your birthday tonight,' he added.

'Birthday party . . .! What am I—a kindergarten kid?' I said.

'You need to get out. Meet people. Socialize. There is more to life than staying in this hell-hole,' Mahesh said. I had just opened my mouth when he shut me up. 'I am not asking you. I am telling you.'

'Alright . . .' I knew it was useless to argue with Mahesh.

After spending almost half an hour with me, they decided to leave. Kamna hardly said a word during that time. We did share some awkward glances and plastic smiles though. At times, I wondered what my life would have been if I had accepted her love. But then, I brushed those thoughts away realizing that my best friend was now her partner.

'I will be back at 5 to pick you up. Be ready,' Mahesh said as he walked to door with Kamna.

I nodded.

'By the way . . .' Kamna stopped and turned to me. 'When was the last time you shaved?'

'Me . . .' I touched my beard. It had grown too long. 'I don't remember,' I said and wondered why had I not shaved for so many days! Truth be told, I did not care. I did not even remember when the last time I had seen my own reflection in a mirror.

'I think the time has come,' she chuckled.

~

After Mahesh and Kamna were gone, I grabbed my towel and wiped clean the dusty cracked mirror fixed on wardrobe. A thick layer of dust had turned it almost opaque.

I stood in front of the mirror for long and stared in the eyes of a stranger. I could barely recognize myself. Depression crept in as I scanned my face for any familiarities.

'What have I done to myself?' I muttered, spreading my hand on my own reflection. Most of my face was covered with a dishevelled beard that was a couple of inches long. All thanks to chain smoking, my once rosy lips were now severely cracked and sort of dark blue. My cheek bones were visible. I focussed on my eyes, there was a deep, depressed look lingering in them. And not to mention unmistakable dark circles. There was hardly any glow left on my face.

I removed my tee and looked at my reflection again.

My ribs were visible, and I could hardly see any flesh. I touched my chest and counted all twenty-four of my ribs. The fat on my stomach was gone too. I looked like a man who has been left to starve for years.

'What the hell have I done to myself?' I yelled this time, shocked to my core.

That was the moment of sudden realization—an awakening, perhaps. I sat by the mirror for a long time and cursed myself.

I had blown a heartbreak way out of proportion. I had wasted too many days of my life—I had wasted my health, my mental stability and all that hard-earned money sent by my middle-class parents for my education.

What was I doing with myself and everyone who cared about me? I did not deserve that. My parents did not deserve that. The people who loved me did not deserve that.

'All this just because a girl dumped you?'—I asked my reflection in the mirror. It was the same question Mahesh had asked me once. It had no impact on me then. But some questions have impact only when *you* ask yourself.

And that was the moment when I decided—IT WAS ENOUGH.

~

'How do I look?' I asked Mahesh, checking myself in the mirror. I looked so different now—so much like *me*, again.

As Mahesh had promised, he was at my room at 5 p.m. sharp.

After sitting there in front of the mirror for long, I decided to make the change. I went to the nearest saloon and got a makeover. The visit was successful because I now had a medium length textured haircut and closely trimmed beard that simulated some three days of stubble. The blazer that Mahesh had bought for me—shiny black—fitted well.

On the suggestion of the hair stylist, I also wore an American diamond stud in my left ear.

I must say, I looked pretty handsome—after months.

'You . . . umm . . . you know R Madhavan?' Mahesh said knotting an orange tie for me.

'Yes. Of course, I know R Madhavan,' I said with a broad smile.

'You look like the poor version of him.'

'Fuck you.' I snatched the tie from his hands and threw it on bed. 'I hate ties,' I scoffed.

~

'You are late to your own birthday party, Mister,' Kamna said and hugged me as Mahesh and I walked into his apartment. I was reluctant but hugged her back. Mahesh too jumped in. It was like a perfect reunion.

I was expecting only a handful of people in the party, but the place was jam-packed with young guys and girls—mostly guys from the naval college. 'Where's your family?' I asked Mahesh.

'Dad is on ship. Mom has gone to Delhi to see her brother,' Mahesh replied.

'Many-many happy returns of the day, brother,' Sukhvinder, my college mate, walked to me and gave a tight hug. It felt good to see him and many other friends from my pathetically short college life.

'Thanks, Sukkhi,' I hugged him back as I scanned the room for drinks. I had decided to reform but was not yet ready to give vodka up. A box of vodka bottles was lying near a luxurious leather sofa. It was all alone—as if calling for me. I walked over to the box and fished a bottle out.

'By the way, brother, why did you leave college?' Sukhvinder asked, holding two glasses.

'Daaru pi, lavde. Mood ki maa mat chod,' I said and filled the glasses with the crystal-clear spirit. I expected Sukhvinder to be offended and leave me alone. Instead, he laughed and raised his glass for *cheers*. I obliged and tasted the fine drink. *Now that is what you call a birthday.*

I was never a loner, but the last few months of my life

had made me strange. I had become so used to staying alone that the presence of so many people around had begun to make me uncomfortable. I had begun to miss my room.

I poured some more vodka in my glass and searched for an isolated corner. Finding none, I moved to the balcony. The flat was on nineteenth floor and the view of road below—with headlights of vehicles glittering like stars in the rain—was simply breath-taking. I had just taken the first sip of my second peg when I heard Kamna's voice, 'You look good in blazers.' She was standing right behind me.

I smiled and turned to face her.

'I wanted to discuss something important with you,' I said before she could speak further. I had been looking for a private moment with her ever since Mahesh informed me about their relationship, and this was it.

'Sure. What is it?'

'Well . . .' I began and looked at Mahesh who was talking to some of our college friends sitting in the sofa. 'Never tell Mahesh about that night,' I requested. I could not meet her eyes while saying that.

The memory of that night was haunting me with guilt. I feared what Mahesh would do if he found out? Would he be able to forgive me for I tried to get physical with his girlfriend? Although, she was not his girl back then. Still, I was worried.

'I told him already,' Kamna revealed, and I just gawked at her. I looked at Mahesh again, our eyes met for a second and he passed a simple smile. *He knows!*

'I told him because a relationship should never begin on base of lies,' she continued. 'But there is nothing to worry about. We did not cross the limit. And yes—I was not in relationship with Mahesh then. So, neither you nor I am at fault,' she finished with a confident smile. I just nodded. I wondered why I could never fall in love with that perfect girl. *Why was I so dumb?*

'Enjoy the party.' Kamna patted my shoulder and left. I smiled, gulped the vodka peg down in a single sip and walked to Mahesh.

While I was in the balcony, a few more people had joined the party. And it was then when my eyes fell on *her*. I was lost the moment I saw *her*. Dressed in a white, sleeveless top and navy-blue jeans, *this girl* had all of my attention in a nanosecond. I felt an odd sensation pass through my body as our eyes met. *She* had a captivating smile—and *she* just gave one to me.

I beamed.

I stared at *her* for long as I studied *her* carefully. *She* had an oval face and fair skin. *Her* beautiful curly hair was tied in a loose ponytail. A stud shone on *her* nose. And *she* was slightly chubby. In short, *she* looked strikingly similar to Tara!

'Who's she?' I asked Mahesh as that *unknown girl* hugged Kamna.

'Bhosadike, do-teen peg mein hi chadhane lagi? It's Kamna,' he laughed out loud.

'Not Kamna, fuckhead. That girl with Kamna, the one in white sleeveless top.'

'Umm . . . don't know. Must be Kamna's friend,' Mahesh guessed. 'Worry not. It's your birthday party. She has to come and wish you.' He winked.

I waited for more than an hour and saw *her* talk to almost everyone around—everyone except me. I tried very hard to not to stare, but I could not take my eyes off *her*. No matter whom I talked to, my eyes always landed on *her*. I felt butterflies in my stomach every time *she* smiled, or *her* eyes fell on me. I was just staring and just staring at *her*. After a while, even *she* realized it—but that did not make me stop.

'Abey aise Prem Chopra ki tarah mat taad, darr jaegi ladki,' Mahesh said sitting in the sofa next to me.

'It would be great if you *do* something,' I hissed. 'At least ask Kamna to introduce me to *her*.'

'Alright now,' Mahesh left the sofa, smiling at me, and shouted throwing his hands up in the air. 'Let's cut the cake,' he announced and pointed at a beautiful pineapple cake—my favourite flavour—that was sitting idle in a corner.

We had a quick cake cutting ceremony. I did not notice who all were wishing me and giving me a bite of the cake until *she* came and wished me. 'This is Alia, my childhood friend,' Kamna finally introduced us.

'Sorry. I had long classes today, so I failed to get you a birthday gift,' Alia said as she gently shook my hand. I felt goosebumps cover my body. While she spoke, my entire focus was on her perfectly carved lips. She had a stunning mole on her lower lip. It was simply *wow*.

'It's fine. You can meet me over coffee tomorrow—as my birthday gift,' those flirtatious words came out of my mouth even before I could stop them. I did not wish to flirt or speak something stupid, but it was already too late.

Stupid me.

I was cursing myself when Alia smiled. I relaxed a bit. Her facial expressions said she knew I was flirting. 'I wish I could,' Alia said. 'But I am going for movie tomorrow—with my boyfriend.'

Fuck me.

CHAPTER 12

Women have always played a huge role in my life. They were my biggest influencers. For a major part of my childhood, I was Mama's boy. Since my Dad was mostly on truck, I was always surrounded by three women—Mom and my sisters—at home. Then came Tara who ruled my life before and after breaking my heart. In between, Kamna played a part, for a short period of time—but she did. And now—Alia.

Alia Shetty, daughter of the Assistant General Manager of Hotel Sahara Star, was the one who shaped my life after I turned nineteen. Shortly after that weird meeting at my birthday party, Alia and I got along well and became good friends.

Unfortunately, she was committed to her childhood friend—now her boyfriend—Roshan Khatri. While the Tara episode taught me that breakups are painful, the Alia episode taught me that one-sided love is even worse. It hurts terribly to see the person you love, loving someone else. *Gaand jal jaati hai bhenchod.*

Thanks to my risk-taking abilities and the habit of taking wrong decisions in matters of love—I still managed to fall for Alia.

She was strikingly similar to Tara in her appearance—except for those spectacles she wore and her height. She was a little taller. And yes, that spectacular mole on her lower lip was the most attractive part. Truth be told, at first it was her resemblance with Tara that attracted me towards her, but the more I got to know her, the more I realized how different—and better—she was in comparison to Tara.

~

'This was the place where Roshan proposed to me three years ago,' Alia said cheerfully, spreading her arms around Roshan who sat next to her.

I was at Indigo, one of the finest restaurants in Mumbai, along with two couples—Mahesh and Kamna, Alia and Roshan. It is frustrating to sit alone surrounded by couples when you are single, trust me.

Alia and Roshan had invited us for a dinner to celebrate the third anniversary of their relationship.

'Hmm . . .' I nodded, showing zero interest in the love story of the girl I loved.

Mahesh and Kamna knew about my feelings for Alia. And they also knew how rude I could be in certain situations. They had already warned me to be on my best behaviour.

'He is a sweetheart,' Alia spoke again, this time hugging Roshan.

Mahesh looked at me and gestured to me to ignore it. He knew how much I hated Roshan. And that hatred mounted that night. I tried hard to smile all the time during that dinner, but jealousy was burning me from deep inside. The way Alia was hugging Roshan and kissing him repeatedly was killing me. I wanted to murder him. The more she kissed him, the more I wanted to punch him harder and harder.

'So, what do you do?' Roshan—tall, fair, and handsome—asked me as the waiter began serving us the food. Roshan was four years older to Alia and had a high paying job in Carnival Cruise Line. It was an American cruise line and he stayed in the US for most of the year. How I wished the fucker goes back to America and never returns to India again.

For that one question, however, Roshan got two answers simultaneously.

'Preparing for Merchant Navy,' Mahesh replied.

'Nothing . . .' was my response.

'Preparing for Merchant Navy or nothing?' Roshan stared between us. Mahesh did not like to confess that I had dropped college altogether, but I knew it was my reality and I had accepted it.

'I did take admission in a college for Merchant Navy but left it long ago. Now I do nothing,' I said, honestly.

'But why?'

'Long story,' I tried to end that topic. It would spoil my mood. I was already in a very bad mood.

'Because his girlfriend cheated on him and then he went mad,' Mahesh spoke after me. I looked at him in rage.

'Aww . . .' Alia reacted. 'That's sad—and cute.'

Cute? How the fuck was it cute? Bloody hell, it was the worst period of my life. It ruined me completely and now I was finding it so damn hard to pull it back together. How could she call it cute?

Women! Their reactions are weird at times.

'But that is the past,' I commented picking up a piece of chicken tikka with a fork. 'I am exploring some good career options now.'

'Why don't you try hospitality?' Alia suggested.

'You mean Hotel Management?' I asked.

'Yes.' She seemed excited.

'No. I don't want to study anymore. I will look for a job. Maybe in a call centre,' I said.

'Hotel Management is not compulsory. You can directly join a hotel as waiter.' Alia seemed genuine with her suggestion, but the immediate facial reaction of Mahesh said exactly what I felt—*humiliated*.

'Waiter . . .' Mahesh sneezed, almost blowing out the water he was drinking. I saw Kamna pinching him.

'What's wrong in it?' Alia argued, a little enraged. She then took some ten minutes to explain to us that waiters in reputed five-star hotels in a city like Mumbai make good money in tips—something around thirty to forty thousand a month, or even more—and salary apart. I was surprised. I never imagined waiters could earn so much.

The way Alia spoke about waiters felt like she was proud of that profession. And it hardly took me a few more minutes to know—*Why*.

'Roshan too is a waiter in US,' she revealed. 'But he earns in dollars, which gets converted into a good six-figure amount in Indian rupees every month.'

'Are you serious?'

'Yes,' she confirmed and kissed Roshan on his cheek. I hated that kiss. *If I stab him in his cheek with a fork, how many days will I have to spend in jail?*—I wondered.

'Lost somewhere?' Alia asked.

'No,' I said, realizing I had already picked a fork up. 'I

don't mind working as waiter if I have a promising career ahead.' I kept the fork back on the table. 'But is it possible for someone to get job in a five-star hotel without proper qualifications?' I put forward the most important question. *You are never going to get this girl. At least get a job*—I told myself.

'Not easy. You will have to prepare yourself for the interview—many rounds of interviews. But when your friend's dad is the Assistant General Manager of one of the biggest hotels of the city—your chances are very high.' She winked, stopping my heart.

~

After that dinner with Alia and Roshan, Mahesh insisted that I must re-join college and not pursue *waitergiri* at all. But I had already made my mind up. Studying for years was something not possible for me anymore, and the Hospitality Industry looked like a great option to earn in dollars in near future.

I prepared myself for a couple of weeks—never thought one needs preparation for being a waiter—and took another four months to get a job in a five-star hotel. And it was not easy—*even if my friend's father was the Assistant General Manager of one of the biggest hotels of the city,* as Alia had boasted.

My first interview was at Hotel Sahara Star. Since Alia had already talked to her Dad—Mr. Shetty, the Assistant General Manager of that hotel—he gave me an appointment.

Alia had helped me prepare and I was confident. After all, the interviewer was my friend's father—*how could he reject me?*

Nevertheless, my confidence was busted minutes after I walked in. Mr. Shetty did not even take five minutes to tell me hard and flat that I was not fit for the job. 'You don't have a Hotel Management degree, Kunal,' he said. 'And not to forget the zero experience. How can I take you?'

'I understand, sir.' I shifted in the chair. His sudden declaration had made me nervous. 'But what do you suggest now? I am very interested in hospitality. And I don't want to wait for another four years and do Hotel Management. Isn't there a way I can get this job without a degree or experience?'

'I am sorry, dear. You should either have a Hotel Management degree or at least have work experience,' he made it clear. My hopes shattered. But given my past experience in shattering hopes, it took me only a few hours to get back to normal.

~

I hatched a detailed plan after the first disappointing interview and decided to start afresh. *C'mon, I just have to be a waiter. Not a bloody NASA astronaut. How hard could it be?*—I bucked myself up.

It started with getting a job at Mocha Coffee and Conversations, a *sheesha* lounge and café in Bandra. Since I wanted to learn the basics of serving, Mocha looked like the perfect place. Being a café—and not a five-star hotel—it was extremely easy to get a job there.

I dedicatedly worked at Mocha as waiter for few months and trained myself. In those months, I also bought some books on *Food and Beverage Service,* which the students of Hotel Management read, and gathered good knowledge of the Food and Beverage world. 'Being a waiter in five stars is not just about serving. You got to have strong knowledge of wines, cocktails and a hell lot of other beverages and cuisines. The better the knowledge, the more chances you have to get a job,' Alia had once told me.

~

'You are drinking here!' Mayur, the Restaurant Manager at Mocha, hardly 25, said in an almost surprised tone. After my shift at Mocha that night—and feeling humiliated from within after a long day of taking orders from young couples of my age and cleaning their mugs and plates—I had decided to get some drink at a restaurant nearby. Coincidently, Mayur too entered the same restaurant and looked a little puzzled as he saw me drinking fine vodka at a restaurant that would unsurprisingly be unaffordable for a café waiter.

'What's wrong with this place?' I said, shaking hands with him. 'Have a seat.'

'No. I mean . . .' he looked as if struggling to find the right words. 'I mean—what's your salary? Four thousand a month?'

'Three thousand eight hundred,' I corrected him.

'And you are going to spend almost a quarter or half of it today itself?' he questioned.

I did not reply.

'Don't take it otherwise . . .' he spoke again. 'I mean, if you drink at this kind of restaurant—why are you working in a café as waiter? I am confused. Being honest, most of the boys working with us may think twice even before spending money on a glass of tea!'

'I am not working at Mocha for money. I want experience.'

'Why?'

'Because I want to shift to five stars—and then to the US,' I told him.

'Then do Hotel Management. I am sure you can afford the college fees.'

'But I cannot afford four years of my life—already wasted a lot of time,' I said as a waiter came to our table to take Mayur's order.

'Kingfisher Strong,' Mayur ordered and turned to me. 'I don't think you will get job in a five-star with an experience of a café.'

'How many five-star hotels you think are there in Mumbai?' I asked.

'Don't know. Maybe fifty—or maybe hundred. I guess there should be hundred five stars at least,' Mayur guessed.

'Then don't you think I can get a waiter's job in one out of those hundred? You think I am that dumb?' I winked.

~

As Mayur had said, it was extremely tough to enter the five stars. I had to study hard for weeks and memories all those long lists of wines, cocktails, cuisines, sequence of service and God knows what not.

Once ready, I updated my résumé on Naukri.com and started facing interviews. They were torture. Those people in the giant, luxury hotels took *waitergiri* a little too seriously.

I was rejected by eleven hotels.

But I did not give up.

It was in my twelfth attempt that I finally got a job, at the Marriott, a hotel belonging to one of the biggest hospitality groups in the world.

All your talent and hard work is a waste if you give up after the initial failures. You got to try again and again, till you achieve your goal.

The primary reason for my selection was the key requirements of the interviewer. He was not focussed on my résumé; instead, he was focussed on my speaking and presentation skills. I still remember the two questions he had asked me, and they were my answers that finally got me the job.

'So, Mr. Marathe, you are very young—nineteen to be precise. Why do you want to do a job rather than doing Hotel Management?' was his first question.

'Why should I choose education from books when I can learn the actual skills from people like you here in this hotel, sir?' was my reply.

'I am impressed,' he said, adjusting the knot of his tie.

Then came his second question, 'Your résumé says you work for nine hours at your current workplace. But here in a hotel, there may be days when you will have to work even for twelve hours. Will it be fine with you?'

'Fine? I would be happy, sir. In the café I get to learn for nine hours a day. Here, I would get three more hours to learn hospitality every day,' I replied and smiled.

His eyebrows shot up. 'Well, whenever I ask this question to candidates, no one ever says—*no*. But this was the answer I always expected. And by the way, we at the Marriott never ask our employees to work beyond the duty hours—unless it is very important. That question was just a test. And your answer was beyond impressive.'

'So, do I get the job, sir?' I asked with anxiety in my voice.

He laughed. 'Well . . . yes.'

So, finally, I had a job in one of the biggest hospitality brands in the world and found a direction to my career.

Even before securing the job, my plans were set, and they were simple. I aimed for working in the same hotel in the same position for two years, and then joining a cruise company in the United States of America—making minimum three thousand dollars a month, which would be converted to almost one and a half lakh Indian rupees in those days.

That was not a bad career choice. Even students in those Engineering and MBA colleges in India would kill for such a job—*given that they are ready to serve food and drinks to people and clean their used plates.*

CHAPTER 13

'Drop whatever you are up to and come to Borivali,' Mahesh said on call. I was in the staff changing room of the Marriott that evening. My duty hours were to begin. I had just removed my black, apple-cut shirt to change into the hotel uniform.

'I am at the hotel,' I said.

'Fuck it and come to Borivali.'

'Dude, I have joined this hotel recently. I cannot just skip my duty. It is unprofessional,' I said. 'And what the fuck is there in Borivali?'

'Alia,' Mahesh said.

'Coming,' I said without any further argument. Quickly wearing my casual shirt back, I rushed out. When it came to priorities, love was always on top for me. Studies, profession, and everything else always fell back. And I always ended up paying a heavy price for my stupid nature.

~

Within the next hour, I was standing in front of Alia's flat in Borivali. Mahesh opened the door. The moment I entered the flat, my eyes fell on Alia. She was crying. Kamna, sitting next to her, was consoling her.

'Alia . . .' I walked to her. She looked up at me. Her usually cheerful face was sombre, eyes sparkling with tears. 'What's wrong?' I took my handkerchief out and offered it to her. 'Tell me what happened,' I asked again. 'And please stop crying.'

She did not react.

'At least take the hanky and clean your face,' I insisted.

'I don't want it,' she wept.

'Why?' I said sitting next to her.

'Because I have one,' she said in the most innocent way possible. Fuck! She was damn cute. I kept staring at her. Even while crying, she looked spectacular.

'Alright . . . but tell me, why are you crying?'

'Roshan cheated on her. Ditched her,' Kamna said, with anger in her eyes.

Now that was a weird situation. I felt confused whether to feel sorry for Alia or jump with joy. I was in a dilemma. On one hand, the news brought a sudden hope for me. Alia was finally single. But then, on the other hand, I knew how broken one feels when cheated in love. I had gone through it. It is terrible. Plus, it was Alia, the girl who brought light into my dark life and helped me build a career.

'Roshan is in America, right? Like, thousands of miles away. How can you be so sure that he cheated on you?' I asked Alia, finally choosing her happiness over mine. I loved her. And true love is not about your happiness—it is about the happiness of the person you love.

I realized I had not changed as much as I expected. I was still the same emotional fool—unfortunately.

'He called Alia last night,' Kamna said. 'Told her he is breaking up. He also confessed having an affair with his American co-worker.'

'Give me his number. Let me talk to him,' I said. I just wanted to console Alia.

'You think things can be fine?' Alia asked, cleaning her tears. I could see hope in her eyes. The hope I once had for Tara. *Fuck love.*

'Of course. I will talk to Roshan and bring him back to senses,' I had just assured Alia when Mahesh grabbed me by the arm and punched me hard in the back. I turned to him, furious.

'We need to talk,' he said, pulling me out of the flat.

~

'Saale tu sach mein chutiya hai yaa chutiya banane ki acting karta hai?' Mahesh barked as we reached a nearby tea-stall and ordered two glasses of tea.

'The fuck do you mean?' I put a cigarette in mouth and lit it.

'You like Alia, right?' he asked.

'I love her,' I replied, confidently.

'Then why all that drama of talking to Roshan?'

'C'mon, Mahesh. I love her. But that does not mean I will be selfish. You know how much she helped me in getting a job. And now it is my duty to help her when she needs it. That is love.'

'That is chutiyapa,' Mahesh yelled. 'Alright . . .' He took a pause, perhaps he realized that it was not actually *chutiyapa..* 'What you are saying is good. I agree. And I appreciate it,' he continued in a much softer tone as the skinny tea-seller brought us tea. 'But think about it. You love Alia. You care for her so much. And if Roshan actually loved her—he

would not have cheated on her.'

I took a sip of tea. Mahesh went on, 'Roshan is fucking a blonde bitch in America. He—'

'How do you know she is blonde?' I asked.

'Arre bhosadike.' Mahesh threw an angry look at me.

'Sorry. Continue,' I said.

'Roshan does not deserve Alia. You deserve her. And if you really love her—you are going to get her. Period.' Mahesh now looked deep into my eyes. 'Nothing is right or wrong in love as far as the intention is *love*. You have a chance now. Fuck that guy, get Alia, and live the life you always wanted—a life full of love and peace. You will never ever get this chance again.'

Those words of Mahesh were no less than a short motivational speech. In no time, all those self-sacrificial thoughts disappeared from my mind and the desire to get Alia drove in. Every word Mahesh spoke made sense. Huge sense. And I knew what I had to do now. 'Alright then.' I took another drag. 'Fuck Roshan.'

~

'The best way to make a woman fall in love with you is the Plan ADC,' Mahesh announced writing ADC on a white writing board. We were in his bedroom that Sunday. Though Mahesh was now in a committed relationship, he was a big player in his old days, having tremendous experience in wooing woman.

His first order to me was to take a few days off from work and focus on *Mission Alia* completely.

I followed his order.

'Plan ADC—what's that?' I asked.

'It's a three-stage plan. A for *Attachment*. D for *Detachment*. And C for *Commitment*,' Mahesh revealed.

'What the fuck?' I laughed. 'We have to win a girl—not a battle.'

'Love is the biggest and the most deserving battle in the world, my friend. Now shut that fucking mouth up and listen carefully.' He threw the marker he was writing with at my head. 'In the first stage—*Attachment*—you have to be her friend, a caring friend, a trusted buddy. Forget the love and just be there for her *as a friend*. Keep your good-for-nothing male ego aside. Stop being an over-protective asshole. Don't overreact on anything. *Just be a good friend*.'

'I am already her good friend, sir,' I said in a boring tone. My hope was dying. *Maybe his playboy days were just a hype*—I thought taking a sip of water.

'Do you know when she gets her period?' Mahesh asked.

'What . . .!' I yelled and sprayed him with water, accidentally. 'Mad or what? Friends don't know that. Boyfriends do.'

'As if you knew about Tara's periods,' he mocked wiping his face. Those words were brutal. I was speechless. I wanted to tell him that I did, but it would be a lie. I actually did not know about Tara's periods. I realized I was too outdated.

'Just do as I say. Be a good friend—a really good friend. She should share everything with you,' Mahesh continued. 'She recently had a breakup. She needs emotional support. It's a good chance for you. Before some other asshole enters her life—you be that asshole.' He winked.

I thanked my lucky stars and set my ass on the mission.

I made a call to Alia the same evening. 'How's you, Alia?'

Without even paying heed to my question, she fired, 'Did you talk to Roshan?' Her question made me nervous, threw me off my game. I cut the call immediately, scared. She called back immediately. 'Did you talk to Roshan?' she repeated.

'Yes. I did,' I lied. 'I told him that you love him like anything.'

'And what did he say?' I could hear her choke.

I closed my eyes for a moment. *I'm sorry for lying. But I will love you more than that asshole*—I said in my mind and spat out another lie. 'He said he is happy with someone else now. And he wants you to move on.'

'Did he?' Alia broke into tears and disconnected the call.

This time, I called her back. 'Can we meet?'

~

We met at Nirmal Lifestyle Mall in Mulund. I had asked Alia to meet at 6 p.m., but I was there by 5:30 and waited for her with a box of her favourite chocolates. As my eyes fell on her, I felt a pang of guilt in my guts. Her eyes were red—due to excessive crying—most probably because of the lies I had told her about talking to Roshan. I once thought of telling her the truth, but I immediately kicked that thought out.

'No movie, Kunal,' Alia said in a flat tone as I revealed her the plan for the evening—a movie followed by dinner, and then, long drive. Thanks to Kamna that I had some insights about Alia's likes and dislikes. She loved movies, Italian food, and long drives.

'But I already bought tickets,' I said pulling tickets out of my pocket. *Last row, corner seat.*

'Can you please drop me home?'

'No . . .' I looked at her with an evil smile and before she could even guess what I was up to, I picked her up in my arms. She was shocked by my unexpected action. Not just Alia but also many of the people around in the mall stared at me—shocked—as I carried her in my arms and walked to the elevators leading to the multiplex. Thankfully, it was Mumbai, if I had done that in Indore, I would have been cursed, abused, or even beaten up!

I was prepared for a slap from Alia—just in case—but instead, she caressed my hair and pinched my cheek lovingly. 'Alright. We are watching the movie. Now please put me down,' she laughed. 'You are crazy,' she added.

'I know,' I beamed and carefully placed her on her feet.

It was indeed a good start.

The evening went as planned—amazing. After the movie and delicious Italian meal, we headed for a long drive. Thanks to Mahesh for he had given me his car.

As we drove through the Western Express Highway, enjoying the lonely road and the dark sky full of stars above us, I heard a sobbing sound. Alia was crying—third time since evening. I stopped the car on roadside. She needed another session of consolation. 'You got to move on, Alia,' I said.

'It's not easy.'

'I know.'

'Did you forget the girl who cheated on you?' she shook me with the question.

I went mute.

'Did you move on—at least?' she spoke again.

I nodded—not sure if I really moved on. But it was not the time of introspection. It was the time to help Alia move on. 'Yes, I moved on,' I said.

'How?'

'Well. I realized she did not deserve my love—just like Roshan does not deserve yours,' I said and took Alia in my arms.

'How did you realize?' Alia asked and buried her face in my chest.

'Chutiyaape ki khaas baat yeh hai ki ek naa ek din woh aapko khud hi realize karwa deta hai ki aap bohot bada chutiyaapa kar rahe ho,' I said.

Alia chuckled. She still sounded low though.

'You know what?' I went on. 'It is our fault. Our fault that we cry for them. We hurt ourselves for them. We waste our precious time for them. But those fuckers who use us like tissue papers and throw us away when done—they do not give a single fuck about our suffering. They are happy in their own world. They forget us like we were nothing—like we have no feelings.'

'So, what are we supposed to do?'

'We are supposed to show them the middle finger and move on,' I told Alia what I could never do—ironically.

She giggled and fetched a handkerchief out of her handbag.

I started the car, but she hugged me back. 'Can we please stay here for some time?'

'Of . . . of course.' I was a little uncomfortable now, but still managed to spread my hand over her head. Turning the engine off, I looked out of the window, lost in thoughts while my eyes stuck on the dark endless road. After a long thoughtful silence, I looked at Alia. She had her eyes closed.

Gathering some courage, I kissed her forehead. It was not a friendly peck; instead, it was a deep kiss. She tightened her grip around me. Her perfume—rose—was driving me insane. I felt my heart beating faster. I spread my hand on her right cheek and kissed the left one.

She did not resist. Rather, she smiled.

I could feel her breathe as my lips moved close to hers, and then, I kissed her on the lips.

'What are you doing?' she yelled and pulled herself back.

'I love you,' I confessed.

'What . . .!'

'Yes. I love you. And I promise I am not going to ditch you like that bastard—'

'Stop it for God's sake.' She grabbed her head and stooped low in seat. I was shocked with her reaction.

'Am I not good for you?' I asked.

'It is not about being good or bad, Kunal . . .' She now placed her palm on my cheek, lovingly. She gently caressed my cheek as she broke my heart into pieces, 'but I see you as a friend—just a friend. I am sorry but I am not over Roshan yet.'

CHAPTER 14

'Did I tell you to propose to her?' Mahesh asked. He was angry.

'No,' I said.

'Then why did you propose?'

'Because when I kissed her on forehead—and then on cheek—she did not resist.'

'So?'

'So . . . I thought she has begun to like me,' I said.

'This is the problem with you small town people,' Mahesh said. 'You guys fail to distinguish between friendship and love.'

'Excuse me. Indore is not a small town,' I argued. 'It is the commercial capital of Madhya Pradesh.'

Mahesh looked at me, displeased. 'Oh really? Tell me more about Indore. Let us keep Alia aside and talk about Indore. Tell me.' His voice was full of sarcasm and irritation.

'Sorry . . .' I lowered my head.

'Now go to Alia, tell her that you are sorry, and promise her that you will only treat her as a good friend.'

'But—'

'Do as I say.' His tone was furious now. I finally decided to follow his instructions.

Being a good-hearted girl, Alia forgave me without

creating any further scene and we were back on friendly terms. In about a week, even after that little distraction, I succeeded in the first stage. I could now proudly say that I was one of the closest people to Alia.

We talked on phone for hours every night and she started to share almost everything about her with me. It was too hard to hold myself back and not end up vomiting *I love you* again but sticking to the ADC plan—and after fucking it up once—I controlled myself somehow.

One night, while we were talking on the phone, Alia told me that she had strong pain in stomach. 'Did you see a doctor?' I asked, worried.

'No. It's normal. I have periods. It happens during periods,' she said, and I just beamed.

~

'I know when she has her periods. She told me,' I told Mahesh with a victorious smile, closing my zipper. We were in washroom of a mall.

'Good,' Mahesh said, still peeing. 'Now be a good friend and buy her some sanitary pads—with some fresh flowers.'

'What . . .!'

'Just kidding,' Mahesh smiled. 'Good going. But now comes the tough one. Step two of ADC. D for Detachment.'

'Detachment . . . sounds weird. What do I have to do in this step?'

'You have to avoid her,' Mahesh said. 'Do not call her. Do no reply to her messages. Talk as if you are not interested whenever she calls you—and cut the call in less than a minute. And do not meet her. Just pretend to be a stranger.'

'What the . . .' I shouted. 'Are you out of your mind? First you asked me to get close to her—as a friend. And now you are asking me to avoid her?'

'Part of the plan, brother. Part of the plan. ADC.'

'Fuck the plan. And fuck you,' I said. 'I have a better idea. I think I should—'

'You don't have to think,' Mahesh cut me short. 'You have to do what I say. You got to avoid her. And keep in mind—you don't just have to avoid a woman. You got to show her that you are avoiding her. Otherwise, she will soon forget that you even exist.'

'With all due respect—fuck you.' I stormed out of the washroom. 'I am not going to avoid her. I am so close to her now. I just cannot ruin all this. No way!'

'You know what?' Mahesh said as he caught up with me. 'You are in the perfect zone now—the zone for losers like you.'

'What zone?' I stopped and looked at him.

'The friend zone,' he bent a little closer to me and said. 'And if you do not act as per the plan—you are going to stay in this zone forever. A day will come, when she will ask you to help her write love letters for some random guy she will fall for. A day will come, when she will go out on a date with another guy and will ask you if she looks pretty enough for the date. A day will come, when she will be fucking—'

'Enough,' I yelled, almost sweating. 'I will follow the plan.' I had no faith remaining in the plan, but the brutal possibilities Mahesh mentioned were scary, too scary for my imagination.

As per the plan, though with a sad heart, I started avoiding Alia. For whole six days, I did not call her on my own. Whenever she called me, I talked as if I were forced to talk to her. Whenever she told me to hang out, I simply said NO. It was painful—but I did it all.

Finally, the brutal week came to an end and now it was the day for the last stage of ADC—C for Commitment.

'I know what I have to do,' I said before Mahesh could open his mouth. 'I now got to commit to her that I love her, right?'

'This is not so simple, asshole. You definitely have to commit—but, in style,' Mahesh said and explained the final stage of the plan in detail. 'Remember. This is a mind game,' he finished.

The plan—indeed—was brilliant. I was simply mesmerized. I was so excited now that for the first time I felt like kissing Mahesh. This guy had probably done a doctorate in love affairs. He was a genius—and so was the plan ADC.

'By the way, you made this plan?' I asked.

'Nope . . .' Mahesh said. 'Romeo Fernandez made it.'

'Romeo Fernandez?' I wondered.

'Yes . . .' Mahesh said and pulled a thin book out of his pocket. It had awfully cheap quality of paper but an interesting title—*Ladki Pataane Ke 101 Tarike*. Romeo Fernandez was the writer of this book.

'What the fuck!' I laughed.

'Do not underestimate this book, my boy. It is brilliant,' Mahesh said. 'Anyway. My best wishes for the final stage of the mission. Now go and make me proud.' He slapped my butt.

~

'What's wrong, Kunal? Why are you avoiding me?' Alia asked in a nervous tone. We were at Aurus, a sea-side restaurant in Juhu. I had asked her to meet at the restaurant at 8 p.m.

She was there by 7:30—before the time. *A positive sign.* I was thrilled.

She was wearing a sparkling black top and white jeans with a leather belt around the waist, a designer steel chain over it. She was looking prettier than ever before.

'I am going back to Indore, Alia,' I started the conversation. 'Leaving this city forever. Just came to meet you one last time.'

'What . . .!' Alia said, shocked. 'But why?'

I kept quiet.

'I just can't understand what's wrong with you,' Alia spoke again. She looked worried now. 'You are acting weird these days. You don't talk to me. You don't reply properly. You don't meet. How will I know what is wrong with you if you don't share?'

I realized that the right time had come—the right time for final move. 'I tried to be friends with you, Alia—but it's not possible for me. I love you and I can't do this friendship drama anymore,' I confessed. 'I am sorry if I hurt you. I know you consider me a friend. It's my fault . . . my fault that I fell in love with you.' I forgot the next dialogue that Mahesh had told me. I was lost. Everything that Mahesh had said blacked out. I just looked at Alia for a long moment. Her expressions were torn.

'Sorry,' I said and left the chair.

Alia caught my hand as I was about to leave. She stared into my eyes, and then, she smiled. 'And what if I say—I love you too? Will you leave this city even then?'

The plan had worked. Mission accomplished.

~

Alia accepted my proposal on three conditions. The first one was that I will never consider a breakup. I felt like kissing her then and there when she said that.

The second condition was way too cute. She said that I would have to give her five chocolates every day. 'Ten . . .' I smiled.

However, her third condition was like a curse and extremely hard to accept. 'We won't get physical till we get married.' Her words came down as a thunderous shock.

'Are you mad?' I said abruptly.

'Okay. So, you don't want to accept this.' Leaving her chair, she kept her hands on her waist. She looked like a dominating tyrant in that moment. Her eyes turned a little bigger and her face was red. 'I understand. You are also like other guys. You don't love me. It's not love—it's lust.' Everyone in the restaurant stared at us. I caught her hand and pulled her into my lap. 'Shut up, Alia,' I said as I caressed her fingers. 'See . . . if we are in love, we need to do certain formalities.'

'Like?'

'Like expression of love and affection with some physical actions,' I tried to explain my intensions in confusing words so that she does not get them at all. As they say—if you cannot convince them, confuse them.

'One word,' she asked.

'Sex,' I barked out. I had no other option left.

Slap!

'I think you are not my kind of guy,' she burst out in anger and got up off my lap. 'Goodbye. Leave the city if you want to. Get lost.'

'You speak a lot.' I pulled her back into my lap. Everyone was staring at us, but I avoided them, my entire focus was on my love. I observed her carefully. The mole on her lower lip was simply breath-taking. I slowly wrapped my hands around her. She was soft—like a new-born. I could see deep innocence in her eyes. 'I love you, Alia,' I said and kissed her, on the lips—in a restaurant filled with at least 50 people. She pushed herself back for a moment and looked deep into my eyes.

And then, she hugged me back, speaking the words I was dying to hear, 'I love you too, Kunal.'

CHAPTER 15

Once again, I had the thing I always wanted—*love*. The two-week-long leave from work that I got sanctioned was over, but I wanted to spend some more quality time with Alia. There was so much I wanted to know about her, so much I wanted her to know about me.

My Restaurant Manager was not an easy-going person, getting that two-week-long leave was not easy. And now, getting an extension was almost impossible. But once again, my dear friend Mahesh came to the rescue. He got a fake medical certificate made for me and I was on cloud nine.

In the next three days that Alia and I spent together, I realized she was the best woman any man could get. She was caring, sort of possessive—which I loved—and extremely innocent. I loved the way she got angry at small issues, but that anger would always end with a chocolate and a smooch.

With Alia in my life, all the damage done by Tara was getting repaired. My alcohol consumption went down drastically—from a peg every hour to a couple of pegs per day—and Alia also made sure that I did not smoke more than three cigarettes a day.

It was safe to say—life was perfect, again.

But then, there are a few people who are born with the most fucked up luck ever. People who do their best—but get screwed again and again because of *luck*.

I was one of those people.

On the fourth day of our relationship, I convinced Alia to stay with me all night. She lied to her parents that she would be staying at Kamna's place and we reached my room at around 10 p.m.

'This place is weird, you have to move,' Alia complained looking around.

'I will.' I grabbed her from behind and kissed her neck.

'Shift to Borivali, near my place—please.' She turned to hug me.

'Alright,' I said and took my phone out of pocket. Making a call to Bilal, I told him to pass the message to my landlord that I would leave that room on the last day of the month.

'But why, brother?' Bilal asked.

'Because I am shifting to Borivali,' I said and cut the call.

'I love you.' Alia kissed my lips. The soft kiss was soon turned into a heavy smooch and I pulled her in bed. It made an irritating sound as we fell into it. It was too weak for two people. 'And you got to get a new bed too,' she laughed.

We kissed again. She was lying over me. I could feel she was breathing heavily. A long kiss later, my hand—that was on her waist—reached inside her jeans.

'Hey . . . stop.' She rolled down from me.

'Why, baby?' I covered her body with mine. I was losing myself. I kissed her neck.

'We are not having sex before we get married.' She pushed me away. 'I already made it clear.'

'Alright . . .' I pulled myself together and fished a packet of Marlboro Hard and lighter from below the mattress. I had a habit of keeping it there.

Soon after I placed the cigarette between my lips, Alia jumped back over me. 'Why do you need a cigarette when you have me?' She snatched the cigarette out and placed her lips on mine. I held her and broke the kiss.

'I will be honest, Alia. You are sitting on a very sensitive part. Plus, when you kiss me, it becomes really hard for me to control myself,' I confessed. 'So please maintain distance if you want to be safe.'

She looked into my eyes. 'You will not cheat on me ever, right?' She had seriousness in her tone.

'Never in my life,' I replied with sincerity, and I meant it.

'You will not leave me?'

'Never.'

'Well . . . in that case—I am all yours,' she smiled.

'I know you are mine,' I started but she placed her finger on my lips. And the next moment, she started unbuttoning her shirt. A rush of strange feeling passed through me. With every button, she drove me crazier.

I just stared at her fingers. And after a few tremendously long seconds, I was staring at her bare waist.

Slyly, I looked up, soaking in her perfect body with my eyes. She had a perfectly carved body.

She now sat with her opened-up shirt, her black laced bra teasing my hormones. She must be expecting that I would do something, but I was too shocked and surprised. My expressions must have given away my feelings for she smiled—smitten and dropped her shirt. I saw it fall carelessly next to her heels.

She then let her hair loose. They fell beautifully on her shoulders. I hated that they covered her cleavage. I pushed them back and traced her bra-line with my fingers. She had a beautiful mole on her cleavage too—it was seducing. I let my fingers linger around it.

'I hope you are happy now?' she asked, grabbing my fingers, and kissing them—or if I must say, licking them. I abruptly lost my control altogether and before I knew it, she was in my arms and I was kissing her furiously. I kissed her deeply and when she broke, to catch her breath, I realized I had already pulled her under me, and she was pinned down.

As I kissed her again, I scanned her whole body with my hands. She was marvellous! I wanted to kiss her more, but there was a long list of other things—fantasies—to be fulfilled as well. I lifted her and unhooked her bra. She gave the wickedest smile ever. It was encouraging. I kissed her left shoulder, dropping one of the straps of her bra. She moaned, full of passion. I had just taken my lips to her right shoulder when her phone buzzed.

'Keep doing it—but don't make any sound,' she laughed, trying to pull her phone out from the back pocket of her jeans, which was not an easy task as I was lying on top of her.

I continued with my kisses.

I kissed her shoulder, her cleavage, her stomach—but then, suddenly, her moaning and seductive responses were gone. I heard her talk, but I did not bother stopping—I was busy feasting on her body.

'Yes . . . no . . . it's fine . . . yes . . .' She sounded extremely serious while responding to the call. I thought it was her

Dad on the phone.

After a minute or so, she dropped the phone in bed and lay still. I was expecting her to moan again, wrap her arms around me, encourage me to go on—but she went rigid.

'What's wrong?' Her expressions drained me of all the erotic feelings I was having in the moment. I saw a tear escape her eye and disappear in her hair. 'Hey . . . what's the matter?' I asked, worried, quickly sitting up.

She sat back with me and sniffed.

'I am sorry,' she cried and left the bed.

'Please tell me what happened?' I too left the bed and took her in my arms. But she pushed me away.

'Who was on the phone? Your dad?'

She just shook her head dismissing the question. 'I am sorry,' she cried and pulled her shirt from the floor. Before I could understand, what the hell was wrong with her in a single phone call, she began dressing up. 'I am sorry . . . I am just . . .' she did not even finish the sentence and started to run out of the room.

'Alia—wait.' I held her hand midway.

'Please. Let me go. I beg you,' she cried more and more. I tried to pull her to me to hug her and help her calm down, but she pulled her hand back and ran away from me.

A few seconds later, my phone rang. It was an SMS from Alia: *I am sorry. I will call you when I am fine. Please give me some time.*

Panic raced through me—*Why does she need time? Time for what? And who the fuck called her?* Hundreds and thousands of thoughts crossed my mind in that one moment.

I dialled her number, but her phone was now switched off.

Having been left with no other option, I fell in bed and did not realize when I fell asleep, waiting for her call.

CHAPTER 16

I woke up with a sudden jerk as my phone rang. It was still in my hand.

Must be Alia—I thought.

But it was Mahesh. 'Alia is in hospital. She tried to commit suicide,' he said with panic in his tone, leaving me scared to death.

~

I fainted at the sight of her. She was lying unconscious in hospital bed with an IV in her left arm. Her right wrist was wrapped with heavy bandages.

Alia had slit her wrist in an attempt to kill herself. Thankfully, the attempt failed.

As she was still unconscious, I was asked to wait outside the room until she woke up. Having no other option, I just stood by the door and stared at her from glass window.

Why did she do this? We were so happy. And who the fuck called her last night?

~

'You can meet her now,' Mahesh walked up to me and said around four hours later as I was waiting impatiently in waiting area of the hospital. Believe me when I say, those four hours were worse than the time when Tara had dumped me.

'What is this, Alia?' I said as I sat next to her. It was too painful to see her in that condition. She turned her face to her mother sitting in couch. The worried middle-aged lady walked out of the room without any question. Mahesh followed her.

'Why?' I spoke again.

'I am sorry. I don't know what to do. I am feeling trapped,' she cried exhaling heavily.

'Trapped?'

'It was Roshan who called me last night,' Alia said.

I felt my blood boil when I heard that name. Two feelings ran through me—anger and panic. *Now where the fuck did this Roshan come from? Was life playing some weird game with me?*

'Roshan said that he realized his mistake and wants me to give him one more chance,' Alia continued. I wanted to murder that son of a bitch.

'So what? You should have told him NO,' I said. 'Tell him that you don't love him anymore. Tell him that you love me. Why did you harm yourself just because that bastard wants to come back in your life?'

'Because we were together for long,' Alia said with teary eyes.

No fuck!

Her answer was enough for me to understand that she was still in love with Roshan. My love of a few days—no matter how true—had failed in front of their long relationship.

Screw that bastard. I am your boyfriend now. I will love you a lot. I will love you so much that you will forget that asshole in a few days. Please don't leave me. I love you a lot. I love you like anything—I wanted to tell Alia. I wanted to scream. I wanted to beg. I wanted to cry. But I did not. I could not.

It was a matter of her life and I could not risk it. She had already attempted suicide once. We were lucky that she was saved. And now, I was worried that if I pressurised her to be with me—burdened her further—she would attempt it again.

'But why did you try to kill yourself?' I finally managed to speak, calmly and politely, while my inner self wanted to scream. 'You should have talked to me about this. We could have found a way out.'

'There's no way out.' Another tear escaped her eyes. 'I committed to you, but I could never forget Roshan. And now when he wants to come back in my life—I am confused. I can't forget him, but then, I can't ditch you too. God! I am trapped.'

'You love him?' I asked. *Please say NO, please say NO, please say fucking NO.*

'Yes,' she said. *Dammit! Motherfucker, son of a whore—Roshan.*

'Okay . . .' I said as I braced myself for my own words. 'Then be with him. There is no confusion. It has just been a few days that we are together. Just forget these days—as if they never happened.' Though I knew I would never forget them.

She stared at me wide-eyed. She perhaps could not believe that I said so, that I was letting her go so easily. 'Kunal—' she started but I cut her short.

'But I want a favour for this sacrifice.' I faked a smile as I stood up. I just wanted to make her feel light-hearted. I knew how hard it is to be burdened with guilt.

'Anything . . .' Alia responded with a heavy voice.

'Never try to harm yourself again. Your life is more precious than these stupid confusions.' I wanted to say some more preaching lines, but abruptly, I felt that the dam of my tears was about to break. I ran out of the room—to cry. And I did not want her to see me cry.

Walking into a washroom, very close to the ward, I literally howled, banged my head to the wall, and kicked the ceramic urinal until a ward boy grabbed me from behind. But what shocked me the most was—I did not cry, even when I so damn wanted to. Rage and frustration had overtaken my tears.

'Fuck,' I yelled again and kicked the urinal one last time, breaking it down, along with a couple of bones of my leg.

~

'That motherfucker had an affair with his co-worker in America. He dumped Alia. He broke her heart. And now when she was happy with you, he wants her back,' Mahesh yelled into space. We were back at my room—with my broken heart and fractured leg—and Mahesh was pacing up and down. 'Is this some kind of joke?' he yelled again.

'Life is a joke—a bloody joke,' I said staring at him.

With Tara gone, and now with Alia gone, I turned to the trustworthy love of my life—my precious vodka.

Mahesh spoke nothing until I emptied almost a quarter of the bottle in one go and he finally snatched it from my hold. 'Kamna told me that Roshan is coming back to India tomorrow—to see Alia,' he said. 'You don't worry, Kunal. I will grab that fucker at the airport itself, beat the shit out of him and make him take his sick ass back to America.'

'Calm down. Chill . . .' I passed a nervous laughter and snatched the bottle back from his hands. 'It's over, Mahesh. Alia is gone. Let those kids be happy.'

'And what about you? What about your happiness?'

'I am used to living without happiness now,' I said and lit a cigarette. Truth be told, I was dying from within. *'Agar naseeb mein ghanta hi likha ho, toh kitne bhi haath per-maar lo . . . end me haath me ghanta hi aana hai.'*

'I seriously feel we should murder that Roshan,' Mahesh went on.

'I seriously feel you need to chill,' I said when we heard a knock on the door. Mahesh walked to the door as I grabbed the vodka bottle again for another sip, sitting in the bed.

As the door opened, Bilal stood outside, smiling, along with an unknown man. 'Hey bro. You are vacating the room on thirtieth, no? This gentleman wanted to see the room—if you don't mind.' His words hit me like a thunderstorm, as if he were teasing me, as if life was teasing me. It reminded me of my previous night with Alia when I was so happy and was about to shift to Borivali for her.

I looked at Bilal, my temper shooting to abnormal highs, and I screamed like I had never screamed before, throwing the vodka bottle at him, *'Bhaag, bhosadike.'*

FULL CIRCLE

CHAPTER 17

I showed a lot of maturity after my love story with Alia died a brutal death. Though the gap she had left in my life could not be filled even after months, and her separation reopened wounds that had never actually healed—it still did not affect me as much as the Tara episode did—not even half of it.

I realized something strange in that phase—and I was not sure whether it comforted me or bothered me—*I was not as crazy for Alia as I was for Tara.*

I still missed Tara.

As far as my professional life was concerned, I was doing better than I had expected. My waiter's job at the Marriott had not only assured me a bright future in the US but also made me unexpectedly good money in tips in the present. And I had a car now—a Hyundai Accent. Yes, it was a seven-year-old second-hand car—but it was still a car!

In short, I was earning well at the age when my friends were still in colleges. Even at the Marriott, I was the youngest waiter. Yet—I was a broken man from within.

I laughed at jokes, wore a plastic smile, and did everything a perfectly happy man would do, but all that was limited to my duty hours in the hotel. Once I took my uniform off and stepped out of the hotel, I was a man no one could stand for more than a few minutes.

I had become blunt, offensive, and exceptionally short-tempered.

'I am jealous of you, bro. You are making handsome money at this age,' Mahesh said. We were on the upper deck of a small passenger boat—known as *ferry*—to the Elephanta Caves, one of the most famous tourist destinations of Mumbai, a network of sculpted caves roughly ten kilometres away from the Gateway of India.

I loved visiting that place. The boat journey lasting for thirty odd minutes—passing through the Arabian sea—had sort of became my hobby. I usually forgot all my sorrows as I looked down into the sea. The endless blue carpet had become my solace and I felt as if it knew and understood my pain despite my silence.

'Great. So why don't you leave the college and join me as waiter,' I said, deeply irritated.

I was in a good mood earlier that morning. It was a sunny day and my weekly off. I forced Mahesh to take leave from college and accompany me to the Elephanta Caves. We had a delicious breakfast of my favourite *misal pav*, treated ourselves to a couple of beers, took a parcel of *vada pav* for the journey, and set off in the boat. Everything was going perfectly fine until my eyes caught a couple standing in corner of the boat—and they were pissing me off to my limits. *Watching a happy couple worked like Viagra to my hormones responsible for causing frustration.*

Mahesh replied to my sarcastic suggestion of joining me as waiter with laughter, but I had completely missed it. My focus was on this couple—two college kids who had most probably bunked their classes and were locked in an air-tight embrace.

'Oye,' I yelled at them. *'Public place hai, bhosadiwaalon. Kya chutiyapa laga rakha hai?'*

The couple broke the hug instantly. The girl was as red-faced as a ripe tomato and the boy looked extremely furious at me. He glared angrily and my first thought was to throw him overboard.

'What the fuck, man! Let them enjoy,' Mahesh interfered, and he also apologized to the highly romantic couple on my behalf. I turned back to enjoy the beauty of the sea and lit a cigarette. My mind, however, was still stuck on the couple. They ignored and forgot my comment as instantly as I had made it, and now they were back in their romantic bubble. The way they were talking—extremely romantically—the way they were cuddling, the way they were laughing together—lost in love—it was turning me more and more pissed and jealous. I was trying hard to avoid them and concentrate on my beloved sea journey, but it was proving to be almost impossible for me with every passing minute.

'Anyway. Why are you doing night duty these days? Change it to day shift. You got to sleep at night, Kunal. Your dark circles are clearly visible.' Mahesh scanned my eyes with a deeper look. He had probably guessed my uneasiness and wanted to distract me from the couple.

'Bhosadike, main waiter hoon, manager nahin. Who does which shift, depends on the manager—not on me.' I took a deep puff and covered my eyes with my newly bought Ray-Ban Aviator sunglasses. My last sunglasses broke a week ago when I had sudden fits while I was buying some shirts in the Fort area. Ironically, those unexpected fits brought more emotional pain in comparison to the physical pain. Right after I used to come out of them, I was haunted with

the memories of the day when I had proposed to Tara in school—I had fits that day too. Those memories were more tormenting than the horrible shakes my body used to have during fits.

'By the way, what happened about your certificate course from Singapore? You told me last week that you would do some shitty naval course of a month from there,' I asked Mahesh. He had informed me about the course few days ago but never spoke about it later.

'Forget it . . .' Mahesh replied.

'Why? Any problem?' I asked.

'It's way too expensive,' he sighed as he fixated his gaze at the sea.

'Your father is a rich man. Why would you care?' I could not help but laugh sarcastically.

'He is rich, but he is a miser. I wonder what he would do by hoarding all his money?' Mahesh continued furiously. 'And I am not on good terms with him. I informed him about this course, and even before I could ask him for money—he gave an outright NO.' He snatched my cigarette and was about to take a puff but threw it away immediately. Thankfully, he realized he had quit it long ago. 'Bloody hell. My father wants me to study only in India and suck it up like he did,' he added.

'Maybe he is right. Maybe you don't need to do that course from Singapore.'

Mahesh gave me a sharp glance. His murderous stare made me flinch. 'He is not,' he said. 'He is old-school. He thinks that since he managed to do it all on his own from here in India, I too won't need it. But times have changed and it's tougher now—the competition is so fierce. If I do that course from Singapore, I will get the edge I need. It will be great for my career.'

'How much money you need?' I asked.

'A lot . . . three lakhs.'

'That's huge,' I had just said when I heard the couple giggling again. I turned, angry, and was shocked to see them lip-locked. If I was angry at the sound of their laughter, their current state made me furious like hell. 'What the fuck . . .' I mouthed and stormed to the other end of the boat, towards the couple. And before Mahesh could stop me, I caught the guy by his collar and pushed him out of the boat—in the sea.

So that was my first night in police custody.

~

'You mean to say—you threw him in the sea just because you got pissed-off?' a senior Police Officer in Colaba Police Station, Inspector Anand Pandit, asked me the next morning.

The boy I had pushed in the sea was quickly rescued by boat operators and I was immediately arrested at the Gateway of India as the boat operators turned the boat back and reported the incident to police.

'My apologies, sir,' Mahesh interfered, keeping a brown envelope on table with cash in it. The Head Constable on duty last night—who allowed me to smoke thrice with a humble bribe of five hundred rupees—had asked for twenty thousand to be free without an FIR. He also assured me that his senior will convince the parents of the victim to take the complaint back.

After a polite negotiation, which included a lot of pleading and begging by Mahesh, the cops had finally settled for half of the amount. *Indian cops are very understanding*—I tell you.

'Actually, sir, he has some mood swing issues,' Mahesh continued. 'Whenever he sees a happy couple—he goes insane.'

'Arey bhai aisi koi bimaari hai toh ghar mein baandh ke rakhna chahiye naa isko,' Inspector Pandit laughed. 'Thousands of couples roam around in Mumbai. Will you hit all of them?' he looked at me.

'I am sorry, sir,' I mouthed.

'What sorry? What if the boy would have died?' Inspector Pandit asked opening the envelope of cash.

I maintained my silence as I had no answer.

After counting the cash, Pandit looked at me, still waiting for an answer. I simply looked down and scanned my shoes.

'You know, this happens due to hormonal changes at this age,' the Police Officer spoke again giving me a meaningful look. 'In fact, this is the reason why people used to get their children married at a very young age in our days. *Saala jo karna hai room mein karo, aur ek hi ke saath karo.'* He laughed again. 'You are getting what I am saying, right?'

'Yes, sir.' I nodded.

'What are you getting?' he demanded.

'That this is happening due to hormonal changes,' I murmured.

'Hmm . . .' Inspector Pandit took a sip from the glass of

tea kept on his table. 'Go now. Run away,' he finally shooed us, and I was utterly relieved. If he had continued with his lecture, I might have had another mood swing then and there.

At last, I was a free man.

The cops returned my mobile phone and wallet and as I checked the phone, I got a major shock—or should I say, *another surprise from life!*

There were eight missed calls on my phone since last night—from Tara. *Why?* My heart started thudding in the chest. *Did she realize her mistake and want me back in her life?*—I thought, almost having a mental orgasm. I called her back without wasting another second.

'Kunal . . .' came a low voice from the other end of the phone. She was definitely crying.

'You all right?' I asked.

'Can you please come to Indore?' Tara cried.

CHAPTER 18

I never understood *why*, but Tara was the only woman in my life who had strangely occupied the most special place in my mind and my heart. She was the only woman for whom I could go to any extent—*no matter what.*

There is only one person you come across in your life whom you love in a way that you can never love anyone else ever again. There is only one person you come across in your life whose image clicks into your mind when you listen to the word *love*. There is only one person in your life who becomes your madness.

The secret to a happy life is to never come across that person.

Unfortunately, Tara was that person in my life.

One call from her and I started my car and left for Indore without any second thought. The only stop I made on my way to Indore was to refuel the car. I did not even stop to pee.

After some ten hours of driving, I was standing in front of Tara on Indore's Ring Road.

I cannot say I was happy but seeing her after such a long time gave me an immense sense of peace. Her presence was my solace.

'Thanks for coming,' Tara said with tears in her eyes.

'What's wrong, Tara?' Her tears ruined the moment. The solace vanished and a grim feeling ran through me.

'I am really sorry for what I did to you. I acted like a bitch.'

'Forget it,' I sighed and felt a tremendous urge to smoke. The good old memories of schooldays were back to haunt me, and her teary eyes were not helping the cause. 'Tell me what's wrong?' I asked again.

'You loved me so much. I still chose that bastard Ronit over you.' Her words, though true and in my favour, stung me hard.

'That is past now,' I said, pulling her towards me. She was standing too close to the road and the passing vehicles. 'And the past should always be left behind. There is no benefit in digging up the buried graves.' I looked into the eyes I could die for. 'Now tell me what is bothering you?'

'I had become so blind in Ronit's love that I forgot my limits,' she started but paused abruptly. Tears rolled down her eyes again. 'I don't know how to tell this to you.'

'If it is important—you should tell me straight away. Don't hesitate. I'm your . . .' I stopped before completing the sentence. *What was I up to?* 'Friend,' I finished.

My words might have stirred something in her because her soft sobs turned into heavy cries. I was clueless to what should I do. Should I hug her, console her, pat her? Unsure, I just stayed mute. She took five minutes to control her crying and then five more minutes to reveal something gruesome—something horrible—something that made me feel nauseated.

'I often bunked my lectures and spent those hours with Ronit in his room.' The first sentence she spoke hurt me as if I was stabbed in the stomach. I was already aware about it but hearing it from her was completely different. 'And . . . you know, all those things happened,' she hesitated, but she continued. I kept listening to her, praying to the Gods that she should shut up. 'But one day, when I fell asleep on his bed, he clicked some pictures of mine—vulgar pictures. And now he is . . . he is blackmailing me.' She continued to cry, and I just stood there, like a statue. A few passers-by stopped to look at us.

I was speechless. I did not know what to say. I had gone numb, as if someone had clicked my nudes.

'Kya hua, madam? Yeh ladka pareshaan kar raha hai kya?' said a young man as he stopped his bike close to us.

'Nikal naa, madarchod,' I told him, irritated. He started his bike and left the spot.

'I feel like committing suicide,' Tara cried again and banged her head on my car door. 'I think this is my punishment for what I did to you.' She was howling now.

'Hey . . . shut up.' I finally took her in my arms.

'I cannot tell this to my parents. I cannot go to police. Dad will kill me if he comes to know about it.' She hugged me back as she sank down by the roadside. I sat down with her. 'I want to die, Kunal,' she cried.

'Stop talking nonsense. We will sort this mess out,' I promised her. Our eyes met for a moment. I wondered what she saw in them because she cried again.

'How?' her voice choked.

'I will figure it out,' I assured her. 'Go home and relax. I will settle this. I promise.'

'I feel guilty for cheating on you,' she spoke again, still in my arms.

'We all make mistakes, Tara. We are humans—not Gods.'

Once I assured her that I will take care of the matter, she left. Finally, I was able to light a cigarette. After a few puffs, my mind said I should stay away from that matter because Tara had dumped me brutally and was responsible for that pathetic period of my life. But my heart that still had feelings for her would not let me leave her alone in those circumstances.

Fuck this love.

CHAPTER 19

'I knew *Karma* will fuck her one day,' Hari screamed cheerfully when I met him and narrated the entire issue. He was my only friend in Indore whom I could have trusted to share that grave issue with. I actually wanted him to help me in getting Tara out of the mess, but he seemed too busy in celebrating it.

'Shut up, Hari,' I said.

'Oh! Fuck you. That bitch deserves it.'

'I need your help, man.'

'Anything for you, brother. Tell me.'

'Take me to Ronit,' I said as I pointed towards my car. We were standing outside his house and my old but elegant Hyundai Accent was parked only a few cars away.

'You said you work as a waiter, right?' Hari asked checking my car out. His eyes ogled at its sight. It made me feel proud.

'Yes . . .'

'Never knew waiters earn so much!' He caressed the car gently.

'I work in a five-star—not a tea stall,' I laughed. 'I will explain it to you later; take me to Ronit first.'

'Yes. I think we should go to Ronit and thank him for the great work he has done,' Hari declared. I wondered how to make him understand that I wanted his help for doing something totally opposite.

Though Hari's reactions were pissing me off, he was not wrong in his place. His hatred for Tara was justified; he loved me too much and cared for me deeply. It is a basic, untold rule of true friendship—*Someone who harms your friend is your enemy.*

'There is nothing great in clicking vulgar photos of a girl and then blackmailing her,' I said.

'Not until the girl is someone like Tara,' Hari argued.

'No one deserves this, Hari. No one.'

'Fuck it. So, we are going to Ronit and thanking him, right?'

'No. We are going to Ronit and kicking his ass,' I revealed.

'What the hell! Why?'

'We need to get those photos deleted. And we need to make sure that Ronit never blackmails Tara again.'

'I am sorry, buddy. Neither I am doing it—nor letting you do it. Never.' Hari looked too serious with whatever he said. He rarely looked serious. 'Did you forget how you cried for her? And did you forget her reaction to your pathetic condition? Don't be a fool again, Kunal. Go back to Mumbai. Just go back.'

'Alright. Thanks for your precious time. I am doing it myself then,' I said and sat back in the car. That was the only way to make Hari do what I expected him to do without arguing further. I was sure he would jump in the car watching me leave.

And he did.

'Fuck you,' he said, adjusting himself in the seat next to me. 'I am doing this for you—only you. I hate that bitch.'

'But I love you,' I smiled and started the car.

'And I hate you too.' He punched me. 'What are his demands, by the way?'

The question made me realize that Tara had left that part out. *Why was Ronit blackmailing her? What were his demands?* My blank expressions made Hari nod his head helplessly.

'You are a fool,' he hissed.

'Are you still friends with Ronit?' I asked after a few seconds.

'Never talked to him after that bitch dumped you for him.'

'Alright. So, today's the day of your reunion.'

~

As per my instructions, Hari made a call to Ronit and asked him to meet. The bastard was reluctant initially, he also asked how come Hari remembered him after so long, but when he was told about free drinks with old friends, he agreed.

In next thirty minutes, Ronit was with us—in my car—dressed in stupid-looking funky clothes—skinny jeans and a Che Guevara T-shirt. The first time I saw him, I broke into laughter. He looked too girlish. With milky white skin and a skinny body, his looks made me wonder why Tara dumped me for him!

'Hey buddy, this is Ronit,' he introduced himself to me and offered his hand for a handshake. Hari told him I was his cousin. We were on the way to Super Corridor, a road that was under construction and almost deserted due to ongoing construction of a railway over-bridge on one of its end.

'I'm Kunal.' I shook his hand lightly as I drove. He laughed listening to my name.

'You find my name funny?' I asked.

'No, no. Just remembered another Kunal. My ex dumped that asshole for me,' Ronit said. 'Never saw him though. He was Hari's friend. His full name was Kunal Marathe. What's your full name, by the way?'

I smiled and stopped the car. 'Hari, can you please drive?' I requested Hari—avoiding Ronit's questions—and got into the rear seat, next to Ronit.

We reached the Super Corridor soon. The place was dark with hardly a few streetlights, isolated and perfect for what I was about to do.

'So, Ronit, you like vodka?' I took a bottle of vodka out from my bag. My car always had vodka, even if it had no petrol.

'I can die for it.' Ronit snatched the bottle from my hand.

'Good. Maybe I will test you for it,' I smiled, and he just looked at me. He had no idea of the gravity of the situation. 'Ever drank a complete bottle of vodka in a single sip—neat?'

'Mad or what? It's vodka, not beer.'

'Hmm . . . drink it,' I said, and his expressions changed. 'Complete bottle. Without a pause. Neat.' I had seriousness in my voice, my eyes staring coldly. 'Drink it now.'

'What the fuck, bro! You are kidding, right?'

'*Bailgadi chala raha hai, Hari?* Gear up,' I said and then focussed on Ronit again. 'And you . . . you drink the vodka. Single sip.'

'Are you out of your mind?'

'*Bhenchod* . . .' I slapped Ronit hard. 'Drink it—now.' The slap shook him well; his head hit the window with a huge bang. 'Do it or I will slap you again,' I shouted. The helpless bastard was in tears now. I could see his legs shaking and eyes widening with fear.

Terrified, he opened the bottle and placed it on his lips. He waited for a moment hoping I would ask him to stop, but instead, I pushed the bottle in his mouth. Having no other option left, he started taking the vodka in. I expected him to fight back after being slapped, but he turned out to be too cowardly to do so.

'If you stop, I will push you out of the car,' I warned him and looked at the speedometer. It was over a hundred kilometres per hour.

The bastard had hardly finished quarter of the bottle when he began coughing heavily. 'I can't drink more. Please let me go,' he cried.

'Alright. Coming to the point now—you have some photos of Tara,' I said lighting a cigarette.

He looked at me in fear. 'You are . . .?' He definitely figured out who I was.

'Where are the photos?' I asked.

'Which photos?'

I slapped him hard again. 'Look around. If I kill you and leave you here in the middle of the road—no one would find out till the morning. Maybe dogs will feast on you, which, to be honest, would be too bad for the dogs.'

'Hari, take me back home,' Ronit begged grabbing his shoulder.

'Answer his question, brother. That is the only way you get to go home. Trust me, this guy is mad,' Hari scared him further.

'I really don't have any photos,' Ronit said in a scared tone.

'Are you sure?' I asked.

'Yes. I swear,' he lied very unconvincingly. It pissed me off even more.

'Alright, motherfucker.' What I did next was pure adrenaline. I grabbed Ronit's neck and pushed him against the door. The bastard was so terrified that he did not even struggle. He was staring horrified into my eyes, and without another thought, I opened the car door and pushed him out—threw him out.

A loud thud and high-pitched scream filled the air.

'Abey chutiye, kya kiya?' Hari yelled and pushed hard on the brakes. 'You said you will only talk.'

'Chill . . .' I stepped out of the car. Hari too jumped out and ran towards Ronit who was now lying on the road, screaming in pain. I checked around to see if anyone was there.

We were all alone.

I walked to Ronit, the burning cigarette still in my hand. I wanted to rub it on his face, but I resisted. His clothes were torn, hands and legs had blood-filled scratches and one of his shoes had fallen off. He was badly hurt, though not fatal.

'We should take him to hospital,' Hari said, worry creased his face.

'Where are the photos, Ronit?' I sat next to Ronit in the middle of the road. A couple of stray dogs walked towards us.

'He will die,' Hari yelled.

'Not yet.' I took a puff and blew the smoke in Ronit's face. It had scratches on the left side. 'Photos?' I demanded.

'They are in my phone. H-h-here,' Ronit slurred and took out his phone—an iPhone—with shaking hands. I had heard a lot about iPhones and had seen many guests and managers in my hotel using them, but it was the first time I got to hold one in my hands.

'How does it work?'

His hands were trembling while he unlocked the phone and opened the image folder.

I was disgusted and filled with rage to see those photos of Tara. I slapped him again, this time, harder than ever.

'Do you have a copy of these photos somewhere?' I asked, pulling him by his hair.

'No. These are the only photos I have.'

'You sure?' I pulled his hair harder.

'I swear upon my mom. These are the only photos I have.'

'Alright. Now listen . . .' I grabbed him by his neck. 'If I come to know that you are blackmailing Tara again—I will kill you. And I swear upon *my* mom, I will. I hope that now you very much believe that I can kill you.'

'Now let's take him to hospital,' Hari hissed.

I avoided his suggestion and looked at Ronit again. 'And if you tell anyone that it was me who threw you from a running car—remember, I have your phone and the photos with me. I won't think twice before revealing that you were blackmailing a girl. Trust me, we both will end up in jail if you open your mouth.'

'Should we take him to hospital now?' Hari asked again.

'No.' I stood up and kept the iPhone in my pocket.

'I am not leaving him alone here,' Hari protested.

'Of course, you are,' I said as I dragged him towards the car.

'You are a psycho,' Ronit opened his mouth as we walked a few steps away from him.

'No . . . I am Kunal Marathe, the asshole your ex dumped for you.' I winked with the most notorious smile and walked away.

~

'You are really a psycho,' Hari yelled as I took a U-turn and drove towards the city. 'What if he dies?'

'C'mon. Those injuries are not at all fatal. He will definitely spend good time in hospital—but won't die.' I picked the bottle of vodka from the rear seat and took a sip. 'And if he dies, just in case, we will have one motherfucker less on the planet.'

'All this for the one who cheated on you?' Hari asked.

'No. All this for the one I loved,' I replied.

CHAPTER 20

Ronit was finally taken to hospital later that night. Some good fellows found him wounded in the middle of the road. Hari told me that the bastard had overall twelve fractures in his body. *Well deserved.*

As expected, Ronit was too terrified to take our names, so we were in the clear. He lied to the cops that he was drunk and took a lift from some unknown men, and they threw him off the car.

'This is his phone. There's nothing to worry now,' I told Tara and threw Ronit's iPhone on the table when I met her the next noon at Bistro Beach, one of the most famous sheesha lounges of Indore.

The place was dark with dim blue lights, overshadowed with sweet smoke from sheeshas. The best part of the lounge was that it was divided into chambers and there was lot of privacy in there. Standing in the middle of the lounge, or sitting in a chamber, it was nearly impossible to peep inside any other chamber.

'I found out that Ronit had an accident yesterday,' Tara said and picked the iPhone up. 'Did you . . .?'

'Forget it,' I said as the waiter brought a Ferrero Rocher milkshake for Tara and a Red Bull for me. She was too worried to order anything. But having known her since schooldays, I knew she loved Ferrero Rocher. 'He will never dare to blackmail you again. And if he ever does, I am just a call away.' I smiled. Tara now seemed relaxed. She passed a soft smile.

But as soon as she checked Ronit's iPhone, that beautiful smile vanished. She was in tears when she checked those photos. 'Bastard . . .' she mouthed.

I felt bad for her. And I also felt that had I not left her alone in Indore and moved to Mumbai, this day would have never come into our lives. *It's all my fault*—I told myself.

I could feel my heart beating faster.

I wanted to spend some more time with her, but I was afraid I would end up saying *I love you*. Deep down, I knew she would accept if I proposed to her in that moment, but that would not be for love—but out of debt. And I wanted her love—true love.

Time to leave—I told myself and patted her back lovingly. 'Anyway. Stay happy. And next time, choose your partner carefully. This world is full of bastards,' I told Tara and left the couch.

'The one I chose in school was perfect,' she said as soon as I turned to leave the chamber of the lounge. I turned back to her. She too had left the couch and was standing right in front of me. *Was she talking about me? Or was it my assumption?*

Tell me you love me and kiss me—I wanted to say, but I did not.

'I was a fool to not to understand it then. And I am a fool even today. I don't think I can be happy ever again—unless you are with me,' Tara finally said it. I stared at her. 'Can I get one more chance?' She took a step towards me, our bodies touching each other now.

'And what if you cheat again?' I don't know why, but I asked. Stupid question it was.

'Not in this lifetime,' she said. I remembered those words. They were the ones I told her the day I had proposed to her in school. Abruptly, she hugged me. 'And if I ever do—you can kill me.'

'This is not what I want to hear, Tara.' I broke the hug and held her face, looking deep into the eyes I loved more than my life.

'I love you,' she said. A huge rush of warmth and calm spread all over me. I felt my whole body rise with goosebumps. I took a moment—a long moment—to let those words sink in. And without saying anything, I kissed her, years after I had proposed to her in school.

That was the most memorable kiss of my life. As my lips rolled over hers, I held her by her back and pushed her in the couch. I was lost in her, lost in love. I remember every single moment of that kiss. The sweet fragrance of green apple sheesha from the next chamber, those soothing lyrics of Akon's *I wanna love you* being played in the lounge and that strong perfume she had worn with notes of peach.

That was the longest kiss of my life and definitely lasted for more than five minutes, with none of us ready to leave. We were coiled around each other like matting snakes when a waiter broke our moment. *'Kya sahab? Lounge main ho aap . . . yeh sab kisi hotel mein room lekar karo.'*

~

'You are crazy,' Tara laughed as I removed her top hurriedly. I had taken the waiter's suggestion literally and took a room in the closest hotel.

The receptionist of Hotel Galaxy—a budget hotel—threw a suspicious look at us when we asked for a room. I lied to him and said that I had come from Mumbai and I will be staying in Indore for a day. It was not an absolute lie, but of course—I was not there to *stay*. 'Who is this madam? You both will stay together?' he questioned suspiciously.

In India, if you ever book a hotel room with your girlfriend or boyfriend to spend some quality time together—*or simply to fuck*—you will realize that it is tougher than cracking the IIT entrance examinations.

I took a thousand-rupee-note out of my wallet and kept it on the counter. 'This is for you. We will hardly spend a couple of hours,' I finally told him the truth and winked.

'Room number 204, sir. And charges are twelve hundred rupees—apart from this generous tip,' he smiled and gave me the key without any further questioning.

So here we were, in bed.

I wanted to admire her body but the urgency in me did not allow it. I decided that I have forever to do so and pushed her into the bed. 'I always fantasized about this since our schooldays,' I said as I grazed my lips on her body. She chuckled but soon those chuckles turned into soft moans. It aroused me further.

I kissed her all over and unbuttoned my shirt.

I was speeding up to the actual *making* of the *lovemaking* part when she pushed me abruptly. 'Wait,' she said.

'I can't.' My shirt was dangling by my shoulders and I was hurriedly unzipping my trousers.

'We don't have *that* . . . ' she spoke wide-eyed.

'That?'

'Yes—*that*.'

'Oops. Condom?' The realization made me feel stupid. But I was not at fault; I was single until that morning—why on Earth would I carry a condom?

She nodded, laughing.

I looked down her naked body and the thought of condom evaporated.

'Fuck it,' I said and jumped on her.

. . . and I finally lost my virginity.

CHAPTER 21

'So, your mom was not ill?' Mahesh asked grimly. I was back in Mumbai and was striding across my room, packing.

I had decided to move back to Indore permanently.

Before leaving for Indore from the Colaba Police Station, I had lied to Mahesh that my Mom was unwell, and I would have to leave immediately. I knew if I had told him the truth that I was actually going for Tara, he would have preferred killing me than letting me go.

'No. Mom was not ill,' I confessed without meeting his eyes.

'You lied to me for that bitch?' His tone was much calmer than I had expected.

I nodded in affirmation. I wanted to shout at him for calling Tara *bitch,* but I did not.

'Bastard,' he yelled and punched me hard in the stomach. 'If she leaves you again, don't show your stupid face to me'.

'Fuck, man,' I cried in pain and fell down on floor. The punch was too hard to tolerate. 'What's your problem?' I gasped.

'My problem is—I have seen you in the worst possible condition for that bitch. And I want you to stay away from her. Get any other girl in your life—but not her.' He gave me his hand and pulled me up.

'I got one,' I said. 'But her ex snatched her back.'

'Alia is history. And so is Tara. If these two are the only women you care about, then you should better stay single for the rest of your life.'

'Do you believe in Gods, Mahesh?' I lit a cigarette.

'The fuck this question came from?' Mahesh said.

'Answer me.'

'No. I don't. Gods are a lie.'

'But I do. I have faith in them,' I said. 'Perhaps, Gods sent Alia in my life so that she can teach me a lesson.'

'What lesson?' He was still angry, but I had his interest now.

'A lesson that forgiving is also a part of love. If Alia can forgive Roshan—why can't I forgive Tara?'

'Fuck you.' He stared at me exasperated. 'And why are you shifting back to Indore?'

'Last time I went away from Tara and shit happened. Now I don't want to take any chance. I will be with her now—in Indore.'

'By this logic I should not proceed with Merchant Navy and stick to Kamna's ass here in Mumbai.'

'You are impossible,' I said as my patience was wearing off. I had just resumed my packing when someone knocked on the door.

It was Bilal and he was holding a small wooden box. 'So, finally you are leaving?'

'Yes, brother. Finally . . .' I said.

'I brought a gift for you. A goodbye gift.' Bilal gave me the box.

'What is it?' I checked the box. Considering its size, it was very heavy.

'Open it,' he said, excited.

My eyes were left wide open when I opened the box. It was a gun—a revolver. 'Are you kidding me?'

'You didn't like it?'

'I love it . . . but it's a fucking gun. Is it original?' I took it out.

'Yes—but stolen,' Bilal said, and Mahesh and I exchanged worried looks. 'Remember you told me that you love guns since childhood?'

It was true that I had a fascination with guns since childhood, but I did not remember telling Bilal about it ever. I must have told him when I was crazy drunk.

'Thanks a lot, Bilal, but he can't keep it. It's risky to keep a firearm without a license,' Mahesh interfered, snatching the gun from my hands and gave it back to Bilal. He was smart enough to wipe our fingerprints with his handkerchief before returning it. 'Plus, this guy is mad. He will definitely shoot someone—or maybe himself—if he flips out.'

I was disheartened watching that beautiful gun go away. But I knew Mahesh was right. I did not need one. And it was certainly risky to possess a gun illegally.

'Alright,' Bilal said and hugged me goodbye.

My packing was done in the next few hours and it was the time to say my final goodbye to the gorgeous city of Mumbai and some of the best people I met there. I was excited to settle back in Indore and be with Tara, but at the time of leaving Mumbai, a strange feeling had overtaken me. It was like I was leaving something behind, something I should have taken with me. It felt like I was leaving *home*.

Mumbai definitely has a bizarre charm in itself. It is a place like no other. Yet, since Tara was in Indore—and so was my family—I was happy to begin the new journey.

'What will you do in Indore?' Mahesh asked as I stopped my car in front of his college, the college that was once mine. The memories of my extremely short college life came back to life.

'There are two big hotels in Indore. Looking at my experience, I will easily get a job at a higher post in one of them.' I got out of the car with Mahesh.

'You love her a lot, hmm?' He hugged me.

'More than anything.' I hugged him back.

'Give her my message. If she ever ditches you again—I will take that gun from Bilal and kill her,' he said with a smile.

'You will never have to. If she cheats on me again—I will do it myself.' I winked and smiled. Of course, I was joking.

He laughed. 'Now that's like my boy.' He hugged me again and patted my back.

I fetched a leather handbag from compartment in my car's dashboard. 'This is for you,' I said and gave the handbag to Mahesh.

'A goodbye gift for me?' he smiled—opening it—and looked stunned to find bundles of cash in it. 'What is this! Why so much money! Are you mad? I don't need this.'

'It's not for you, bitch. It's for your course in Singapore,' I said. 'I had one lakh as of now . . . I will arrange and send you rest in a few days.'

'No. I can't take this.' Mahesh zipped the handbag close and threw it back in the car.

I took it out again.

'I am not asking you. I am telling you,' I said. 'You have to keep it. And you have to do that shit course from Singapore.'

'I don't need the money from you, Kunal,' Mahesh argued. 'You are not my dad.'

'That's not what your mom said last night,' I joked, pushing the handbag back in his hand.

Shit! He punched me again in the stomach and walked to the college gate. He had a smile on his face when he turned back to me and waved a goodbye. 'I'm gonna miss you,' I muttered and got back into my car.

~

Before driving back to Indore, I made a quick stop at Bilal's place and took the gift he had offered me. It was a bloody gun—and I loved it.

'Never tell Mahesh that I took it from you,' I requested Bilal.

'And if you are ever caught with this gun, never tell the cops that I gave it to you.' He winked.

'Deal,' we laughed and hugged.

CHAPTER 22

Have you ever been in a phase that you want to live again, and again, and again—in a loop—till the end of the time? The next year of my life was that phase for me.

If I ever look back, it feels like only yesterday when I got Tara back in my life and all those dark times were now a distant memory. I was the happiest in that year. The glow cast by that period was like the mesmerizing sight of a falling star, a sight that is too beautiful to be forgotten till your last breath, but a sight that passes too quickly to satisfy your soul.

Leaving Mumbai was a setback to my career, but I was so happy with Tara that a low-paying job in a three-star hotel of Indore seemed perfect now. Thanks to my experience in one of the biggest hotel chains in the world—Marriott—I soon managed to get a job with a promotion in Indore. I was no longer a waiter. I had joined as an F&B Executive. Still, I did not make half the money I used to earn as a waiter in Mumbai. But I was fine with it. Tara was with me—and I was ready to make any sacrifice to be with her.

Mahesh was the only person from Mumbai whom I missed terribly, and not to mention I owed him big time. I kept my promise of sending him rest of the money for his course—I sold my Hyundai Accent to raise that amount. Now, he was successfully certified with some crappy course from Singapore and was happy with Kamna.

His happiness mattered a lot to me, especially after what he had done for me in the dark period of my life, and selling a car was no big deal for that.

As far as my family was concerned, they were furious to learn that I had given up the naval college and joined the Hospitality Industry. When I broke the news to them, they could not believe me for a few minutes. I still remember their confused, stony faces. However, when they were able to fully absorb what I had said, they almost killed me with their reaction. 'Did we struggle all our life to provide you the best possible education so that you would end up being a waiter?' Dad had yelled at the top of his voice. Mom, too shocked to say anything, had tears in her eyes.

They were highly disappointed with me. And they were not wrong.

I felt terrible for what I had done, but it was all in the past. Nothing could have been done about it anyway—so I let it pass, like many other things.

As the time passed, my family too accepted my new career choice and forgave me for my stupidity. *Parents . . . I wonder, how they can be so generous and kind-hearted towards their kids. No matter what you do, they always find a way to forgive you. They are living Gods, trust me.*

Another good thing I did to myself was quitting cigarettes and alcohol. I now lived a totally sober, decent, civilized life. All the craziness was gone, and I had turned into a responsible man. Anyone who would have seen me during my new phase—saying NO to every offer of smoke or drink—would have never ever believed that I was once a person who could not stand properly without a peg of vodka once every hour.

'How do you guys manage to stay away from alcohol?' Ankur, my colleague at the hotel, once asked me during a staff party. He was having a beer and I had restricted myself to a soft drink.

I smiled hiding my amusement. The situation was hilarious. 'You never tasted alcohol?' He looked dead curious.

'Never,' I lied.

'Dude. Why are you even alive?' he joked, and I laughed. 'Try it.' He almost passed me the beer. I was about to deny it politely when he spoke again, 'Wait . . . Forget it. Tolerating alcohol is not everyone's cup of tea. You know—it's alcohol, after all. I don't want to end up carrying you home.' He laughed and took a sip.

Asshole. Boasting so much just about a fucking beer? I can drink every bottle of vodka present in the hotel and still be able to drop your fucking ass home—I wanted to tell him. But I simply nodded, allowing him to take pride of his so-called *capacity*.

I had begun to love the new me—or was it the old me, before I had shifted to Mumbai?

~

My new routine was simple; busy with my job six days a week, and on the seventh day—my weekly off—reaching Tara's college bus stop ten minutes before the scheduled time of her bus.

I still remember the smile she used to give me along with that sparkle in her eyes seeing me, waiting for her on my newly bought bike—a Hero Honda Hunk. No matter what day it was—as my weekly offs were not fixed to any particular day—she always bunked her college and we used to spend the day together.

Our day would begin with a typical *Indori* breakfast of *Poha-Jalebi* at the famous *Chhappan Dukaan*, the most renowned food street of Indore. Tara loved it, hence I did too. Then we would go to an early morning movie show at PVR in Treasure Island Mall, one of the most popular destinations for *Indoris*—kind of *gareebon kaa Las Vegas*. Luckily, my weekly offs were never on weekends due to the high footfalls in the hotel, and hence, those early morning movie shows on weekdays hardly had a few dozen audience.

Ideally, people visit multiplexes for the sake of watching movies, but it was not the case with us. We went to theatres to take advantage of the darkness it offered. We always chose corner seats . . . and well . . . the rest can be understood.

I hardly remember the story of any of the movies we saw together. At times, we used to go so wild in the theatre that we used to forget that we were not in my bedroom. We were even interrupted by the security staff quite a few times for our PDL (Public Display of Lust). However, once the security person was gone, we would resume exploring each other's body in the darkness.

After the movie, we used to head straight to my home—all charged up after hours of foreplay in the theatre—jumping into the bed straightaway.

'Why did we go to PVR if we had to come to your place?' Tara asked putting her arms around me the first time I took her home. 'We could have come here directly.'

'Because mom leaves for her office at ten-thirty.' I pushed her in the bed.

She laughed before our lips met.

'And what about your sisters?' she asked, breaking the kiss. 'Elder one got married, and the other one stays in hostel,' I told her, removing my shirt. 'Now shut up and kiss me again.' Exhausted with all the love making and with our bodies covered with love bites, we would then have lunch in some lavish restaurant.

Finally, five to ten minutes before her bus would arrive to drop the students at her stop, I would drop her off with a goodbye kiss.

~

I wonder how many would have noticed that there is a major difference between having sex and making love with the person you love. That moment when you take your girl in your arms and kiss her forehead with all your warmth, that moment alone gives more pleasure than a thousand orgasms. It is like your life is limited to her. For that one moment, the world becomes a lie, and your love is the only truth for you.

Tara was the only truth in my life, the only woman I was afraid to lose—the only woman I could never afford to lose.

~

'Are you sure about it? I would suggest you, think once more.' Hari bounced on his heels as he tried to stop me from committing one of the stupidest things in my life.

'I am sure. Now stop bothering me,' I said, irritated.

'I think Hari is right, buddy. Think once again,' the tattoo artist said.

Valentine's Day was approaching, and I had planned one of the best gifts any guy can give to his girl. I was getting Tara's name written on my arm with a permanent tattoo.

Hari was against this decision and had already declared it a foolishness. 'What if she leaves you again?'

'Shut up, Hari. Why are you always so negative?'

'Okay. Fine. She will not leave you. But imagine if you have a fling with someone else in the future—what if that girl finds another girl's name on your arm? It will be such a turn off, bro. You may miss the chance,' Hari had his usual idiotic smile on his face when he said that.

'Really?' I looked at him in shock. 'You are so far-sighted?' I said in a sarcastic tone. He took my sarcasm as compliment and nodded. That idiotic smile was still on his face. 'Now shut the fuck up and let him make the tattoo.' I gestured the tattoo artist to begin.

'Girlfriends may not be permanent, dude. But this shit is.' The tattoo artist showed the tattoo gun. 'If you want, I can make a lion on your arm. Why write a girl's name?'

'Good idea,' Hari spoke again, enlightened. 'Remember, you used to scribble that bull everywhere in school? Why don't you get a bull made on your arm?'

'Make the fucking tattoo that I asked you to—or I am leaving,' I finally yelled at the tattoo artist.

'I can't see this,' Hari said overdramatically and walked out of the tattoo parlour.

I finally took a sigh of relief as the tattoo artist started the tattoo gun.

~

'I can't believe this.' Tara's eyes glistened with tears when she saw her name on my arm. 'Is it a permanent tattoo?'

'Of course.' I smiled and kissed her.

'But—' she had started to say something when I locked her lips with another kiss.

It was Valentine's Day and after a romantic lunch in the newly opened *Radisson Blu Hotel*, we were lying on my bed, having nothing but a blanket on our naked bodies. Like any usual day, Dad was out of the city and Mom had gone to her office. We were alone at my home—of course.

'This is the best gift any girl can get,' Tara said. 'I love you.'

'I love you too.' I hugged her tight. It was like our bodies had become one. It was like there was nothing that could separate us. It was like we could stay there—wrapped around each other—for our entire lives.

And then, doorbell rang.

'Who could it be?' Tara asked, worriedly clutching the sheets. 'Your dad?'

'He is not in town,' I replied.

'Mom?'

'She never comes home before six-thirty,' I assured her and left the bed. Wrapping a towel around my lower body, I walked to the drawing room.

'Fuck!' I mouthed as I peeped through the door viewer. *It was Mom.*

~

'So, this is what happens at home in my absence?' Mom said furiously after I dropped Tara at her place and reached back home. Mom was not even close to this angry when she came to know that I had dropped out of college and became a waiter. 'If I had not taken a half day at work, I would have never come to know about it.'

I said nothing. *Never argue when your mother, girlfriend or wife is angry. It is one of the biggest secrets of a man's happy life.*

'What's her name?' Mom spoke again. Her tone lowered a little.

'Tara,' I replied without meeting her eyes.

'So, what now?'

'I want to marry her,' I said, bluntly.

Mom looked into my eyes—still angry—and left the sofa. I waited for her reaction. She walked towards the kitchen without saying anything. Before leaving the drawing room, however, she turned. 'Bring her home someday—but in my presence.' She had zero expressions over her face. Once again, I felt ashamed of being caught under those circumstances. 'By the way, the girl is beautiful.' And Mom finally smiled.

~

'I am nervous,' Tara said as we stood in front of my flat, all set to ring the doorbell.

It was my next weekly off and as per Mom's instructions, I had brought Tara home. My entire family—Mom, Dad, and sisters—were there. Everyone wanted to meet the girl who had captured my heart and soul.

'Calm down. They are my parents, not your placement interviewers,' I joked.

Tara did not laugh. She threw an angry look at me. Dressed in a maroon *salwar kameez,* she looked exceptionally gorgeous. 'What if they reject me?' She looked cute when she was nervous. I wanted to kiss her then and there.

'Who cares? I am still going to marry you.' I placed a quick peck on her cheek.

She smiled.

Time is a weird phenomenon. When it is bad, it fucks you in almost every way possible. But when it is good, even the hardest of the situations pass away like a cakewalk.

My parents, contrary to my assumptions, were extremely happy to know that their son had found a soulmate. Everyone from the family loved Tara.

My marriage was officially approved by my family.

When Dad smiled and said, 'good choice', and then, when Tara looked into my eyes and blushed, I remembered those gruesome days I spent in Mumbai when I never imagined this day would ever come into my life. My eyes fell on the statue of Lord Ram and Mata Sita, along with Lord Hanuman—the one I always prayed to—and I thanked them for the day, for the perfect life—for Tara.

Life! It's unpredictable.

2011

CHAPTER 23

Minutes before my 21st birthday, on a rainy night, I sat in a vacant guest chair of the poolside restaurant I worked in. Most of the guests were gone and the closing formalities were about to begin.

'Sir, everyone is waiting for you,' Nishant, a waiter and one of my closest boys in the hotel, called out to me. My colleagues had arranged a small cake-cutting ceremony to celebrate my birthday and were waiting for me in room service area.

'Give me a minute,' I said and took my phone—now an Android—out of my pocket. I was waiting for the clock to strike 12 and get the first call from Tara. I knew she would call me before anyone else. I knew she too would be holding her phone and waiting for the special day to begin.

I waited patiently. The countdown had begun. Five. Four. Three. Two. One. And my phone rang.

It was not Tara. It was Mahesh. 'Happy birthday, bitch,' he yelled.

'Thanks, brother,' I had just said when I realized another call was on waiting. *Tara*—I guessed.

Wrong guess. It was Hari this time.

In next fifteen minutes, I got around a dozen calls from my family, relatives, and friends, but none of them was from Tara. I wondered—*Why?*

Maybe her Hitler dad is around—I thought.

While my colleagues—executives, waiters, hostesses, chefs, and trainees—were busy singing the *Birthday Song* and I was cutting the cake, my phone buzzed again. *Tara, for sure.*

Alas. It was an unknown number.

I excused myself from the celebration and answered the call. *'Tharki kaa matlab jaanta hai?'* said an unknown male voice from the other end of the phone.

'Sorry. Who's this?' I asked.

'I am the one who slept with Tara before you could,' the unknown guy said and laughed hysterically. My blood pressure shot up.

'Aye,' I yelled into the phone. *'Kaun bol raha hai bhenchod?'*

There was a sudden silence in the background. I looked back at my colleagues who stopped the celebration abruptly and were now staring at me.

'Calm down, buddy. Ronit here,' the unknown guy on phone revealed his identity.

'I guess our last meeting was not enough for you,' I said, pissed. 'Give me your address. Let's meet again.'

'First you got to answer my question, buddy,' Ronit said. 'Do you know the meaning of *Tharki?*'

'It's my birthday, Ronit. Don't fuck my mood.'

'Alright,' he said. 'Let *me* tell you the meaning of *Tharki*. If we talk about *us*, the men, then *Tharki* is a man who is crazy for women, crazy for sex. A man always filled with lust. A womanizer. A playboy.'

'A man like you,' I said.

'Yes. A man like me,' Ronit laughed. 'But the point is—it is not just men who are *Tharki*. Even women are. Women who just cannot be satisfied with one man. Women who need more and more men. Women who can never be loyal in relationship—no matter what you do for them.' He paused for a moment and spoke again. 'Women like Tara.'

'Just tell me where the hell you are,' I said in rage. 'I am going to come to you. And I am going to kill you.'

'No need to come to me,' Ronit said. 'I'm texting you an address. Pratyush's address. He is—'

'I know who Pratyush is,' I cut Ronit short. 'He is Tara's batch mate. Her good friend.'

'Boyfriend,' Ronit said. 'Pratyush is Tara's boyfriend. New boyfriend. Your sweetheart is cheating on you again.' He laughed.

'You think I will trust you?' I said.

'You will not. I know,' Ronit said. 'That is the reason I am texting you Pratyush's address. Your Tara is spending the night with him. Go and see it yourself.'

'I trust Tara,' I said. 'So, you can just fuck yourself. Don't you dare call me again.'

'Waqt badal jaata hai, mere dost, lekin insaan ki fitrat nahin badalti,' Ronit laughed and disconnected the call.

My phone beeped. There was an SMS from Ronit—it was an address.

I wanted to dismiss all those allegations then and there, and thus, I called Tara. But her phone was switched off.

'Anything wrong?' Ankur, my colleague, walked to me and asked.

'I need your car,' I said, my hands quivering.

~

Dressed in my hotel uniform—white shirt and black pants with stripes—I stood in front of flat number *103* of *Shiv Shakti Apartment* in Bhawarkuan—the address given by Ronit—Pratyush's address. I was sweating so profusely all the way that I had to take the blazer off and throw it in backseat of the car.

I had a fair idea that Ronit was lying and was just trying to get even with me. I had done some permanent damage to his body in our last meeting. *But why is he doing this now? Why after a bloody year?*

I still reached the address. If not for Tara's integrity, then for my own mental sanity. *That bastard was lying*—I told myself and knocked on the door.

'Who's there?' said a male voice, Pratyush's most probably.

I knocked again.

'Kaun hai, bhai?' he said and opened the door. Yes. It was Pratyush. He was dressed in nothing but boxer shorts, upper body naked. 'Kunal . . .?' he said, a little frightened. His reaction increased my insecurities.

Ignoring him, I scanned the drawing room. It had nothing but a mattress, a TV set, and a guitar. Heaving a sigh of relief, I walked in.

'Listen, dude. You can't just walk in,' his tone held an unsaid warning.

'I will leave soon.' I strolled towards the bedroom.

'Hello,' he yelled and grabbed me by my arm. His behaviour was alarming.

'What's the matter? I just want to check your bedroom,' I said in a polite yet threatening tone.

'No—you can't? he stammered.

'Why?' I eyed him suspiciously.

'Because my girlfriend is in there.'

Was Ronit right?—I thought. 'What's your girlfriend's name?' I demanded.

'That is not your concern, Kunal. Get out of my flat.'

'It is my concern,' I roared and rushed to the bedroom door.

'No,' he shouted at the top of his voice and blocked my way.

'Let me check your bedroom, Pratyush,' I warned him.

'Leave my flat—now.' He grabbed me by the collar.

My temper was near the snapping point. I looked into his eyes and waited for a couple of seconds for him to back off. He did not. 'Don't try to fuck with me at this moment,' I hissed and kicked him in stomach.

He fell with a clatter on a few utensils kept in the passage that led to the bedroom.

'Sorry,' I mouthed realizing that the kick was way too brutal, and I tried to open the bedroom door. It was locked from inside. 'Open the door,' I said, knocking on it.

There was no reply.

'Listen, ma'am,' I said, politely. 'Whoever you are. Just open the door. I will see you and I will leave.'

No reply. The door was still closed.

'Alright, say something—anything. I will listen to your voice . . . and I will go away. Can you please speak something?' I requested from the door.

No reaction yet.

The clouds of doubt began to take a greater shape. The girl inside would have at least spoken something, would have at least screamed in fear, unless it was someone who knew that I will recognize her voice, unless it was . . . *No. I am just over thinking*—I convinced myself.

'Pratyush.' I walked back to him. 'Ask your girlfriend to open the damn door.'

'You might have scared her. She won't open the door,' Pratyush said, trying to sit up.

'Fine. Ask her to speak something.'

'I will call the police, Kunal,' he almost cried.

His answer enraged me further. 'You think I am playing, hmm?' Frustrated and enraged, I walked to the small kitchen attached to the passage and grabbed a knife. I was full of doubts, insecurity, and fear—and I literally had no idea of what I was doing. 'Enough of the drama now.' I sat in front of Pratyush, showing him the knife. 'Call your girlfriend out in ten seconds, or I will slit your throat right fucking now.'

He looked at me with terror in his eyes. His lips trembled when he looked at the bedroom and spoke, 'Come out. Please come out . . . or he will kill me.'

I stood up as I heard the door latch opening. My eyes

were fixed at the door. I had never been so restless in my life before. *Not Tara*—I prayed to every God possible.

As the door opened, the rug was pulled out from under me. *It was Tara*—coming out of another man's bedroom. Her clothes said that she had worn them in a hurry. Her hair was scattered. Her face looked full of guilt. 'I am sorry, Kunal. I was about to tell you,' she muttered.

I went blank for a moment.

'Tell me what?' I took a step towards her. My hands, still holding the knife, were shaking.

She said something, but I was not in a condition to listen to anything.

'What kind of woman are you?' I managed to speak, and as I took another step towards her, I almost stumbled. My legs gave in. My hands began to shake rapidly, and I had a spasm in my tongue.

Before I could realize, I had fits, and I fell on the floor. Worse, I fell in a way that the knife I was holding got buried in my body, a little below the shoulder.

~

'No. No one stabbed him,' Pratyush said as the doctor stitched my wound. Fortunately, it was a thin kitchen knife and did not do major damage. But it was painful. 'He was holding the knife when he had fits,' Pratyush went on. 'He fell down. And the knife got stabbed.'

'Why was he holding a knife?' the doctor asked, suspiciously.

'I was cooking,' I lied. Pratyush looked at me and took a sigh of relief.

Soon after I fell on the knife, Pratyush called some of his friends from the flat nearby and they took me to a hospital immediately. The boy was not as bad as I had thought. Being honest, if I were in his place, I would have kicked the wounded guy out of my flat if he was my girl's ex. But Pratyush did not. He took me to a hospital! *Who does that?*

Tara, however, stood there—like a dummy—and just stared at me while the boys took me away. She did not even flinch at the sight of me having fits. She did not even bother to hold me or support me as I fell. She did not even bother to check me as I bled. She just did not bother anymore.

'Where's she?' I asked Pratyush after the doctor left and we were alone in the emergency room.

'I am sorry, Kunal,' Pratyush said. 'Tara had told me that she no more loves you and she just cannot tell you about it.'

'How long has it been going on?' I felt broken from inside and my desire to yell at him was lost somewhere.

'A couple of months,' he replied. I clenched my fists in anger as those words fell on my ears. I sat motionless on the stretcher, my head resting on my hand.

'I am sorry,' he muttered.

I looked at him, helpless and enraged at the same time, and then, I jumped off the stretcher. 'Take your shirt off.'

'Sorry?' He looked puzzled.

'Give me your shirt. I got to go,' I demanded angrily as I tore open my shirt that was soaked in blood. 'And where's my car?'

'It must be parked near my place. Give me the key, please. My friend will get it here.' He began taking his shirt off. He was clearly scared of me.

'Ask your friend to get some bottles of vodka as well.' I threw the key at him. Though I had given up drinking, I needed vodka that night. I really needed it.

'Vodka? At this time?'

I just looked at him in rage.

'I will get it. Give me ten minutes, please.' He ran out of the emergency room.

'Do you even know which car it is, idiot?' I shouted.

'Sorry . . .' He walked back into the room.

'It's a white Indigo.'

'Alright.'

After I was left alone in that room smelling of strong medicines, I leaned over the stretcher and closed my eyes, to calm myself down. I felt as if I was stuck in severe mental chaos. It was too much for me to bear.

Staying there in same position for a few long minutes, I took my phone out of my pocket and called Hari. His phone was switched off.

Then I called Mahesh. 'Take the earliest flight to Indore,' I felt tears building in my eyes when I said that. I stopped them from flowing out. *I am not going to cry again. No more*—I told myself.

'Hey . . . anything wrong?' Mahesh asked in a sleepy voice.

'Come soon, Mahesh. I need you.'

'Yes, I am coming. But tell me what's the matter?' his tone was laced with worry.

'Just come to Indore as soon as possible,' I said.

'Alright. I will be there at the earliest. You—' I cut the call before Mahesh could finish.

~

It was still raining as I walked out of the hospital. Pratyush, who was now in inner vest and waiting for me at the counter, followed me without uttering a word. He still looked frightened.

The car I had taken from Ankur was parked right in front of the hospital gate. 'I could only manage whiskey and rum. No vodka,' Pratyush told me. 'There is one bottle of RS and one of Old Monk. I kept them in your car.'

'Who the fuck drinks RS?' I stopped and looked at him.

'Look at the time, bro. The shops are closed. Bought the bottles in black. Paid double,' he replied meekly. 'I am just a student, bro. That's all I can afford.'

'And still she cheated on me for you,' I said and kept some money in his hand.

'She said she loved the way I dance. And that made her fall in love with me.'

I looked at his stupid face. The guy had no idea that had he not been kind enough to take me to the hospital, he would have been admitted in the same hospital. '*Mujra kar ke pataai hui ladki kitne din tikegi, bhosadike*?' I said and walked to the car.

'Kunal . . .' Pratyush ran to me as I entered the car and wore my black blazer. 'I love her,' he said, standing at the car door.

'Then you will regret it soon.' I started the engine.

'How can you be so sure?' He looked into my eyes.

'Kyunki waqt badal jaata hai, lekin insaan ki fitrat nahin badalti,' I said and left.

CHAPTER 24

I drove aimlessly in the rainy night on empty roads. I had no idea where I was going, I just kept on driving. It was undoubtedly the heaviest rain of the season and the darkest night of my life.

My phone buzzed more than a few times, but I ignored it.

'Bitch,' I finally screamed, letting all the frustration out, and stomped on the brakes. The car came to a screeching halt.

I pushed the seat backwards with shaking hands. My head felt numb. After staring at the roof of the car for long, I closed my eyes.

Taking a deep breath, I closed my eyes and tried to figure out—*What the fuck had just happened?*

'It's wrong.' I opened my eyes and the bottle of Old Monk. 'Not again.'

Tara had made a joke of my love. I had begun to hate her to my core now. In a single night, all my perceptions of true love, blind faith and being together forever were gone—and she was responsible for it.

The love I had for Tara was over. It was overtaken by hatred. And now, all I wanted was to settle my score with her. 'I forgave you the first time. But not now,' I muttered and took a hard pull of the rum.

While a thousand dreadful thoughts crossed my mind with every sip of the rum, I recalled a name—Bilal. I remembered what he had told me the first night we sat in my room in Mumbai to drink. He had served three years in prison for making a false promise of marriage to his girlfriend and then leaving her after a long physical relationship.

As the rum overtook my senses, I started the car again and drove to the nearest police station.

~

'What's troubling you at this time of night?' Sub Inspector Baldev Mishra—as written on his name tag—asked in a disinterested tone as I took seat in a police station. A giant wall clock above the logo of Madhya Pradesh Police indicated that it was 3:10 a.m.

'I want to lodge an FIR.' I looked up morose, as if life had been drained out of me. Totally overpowered by alcohol, I tried my best to look sober.

'FIR for?'

'If a person promises to marry someone, they have physical relationship, and then that person cheats . . . and breaks the promise—what charges can be imposed on that person?' I asked hesitantly.

'Cheating, sexual exploitation, even rape—depending on certain factors,' the otherwise disinterested cop said with an unexpected attention and opened a thick, nearly torn register. 'Where is the victim? Let us take *her* statement and we will arrest the culprit immediately.'

'Actually, sir . . .' I said, 'the victim is not *her*. *He* is a man . . . It is me.'

Mishra looked confused. His facial expressions showed he tried to understand but failed miserably.

'Come again?' He bent closer to me.

'I was in relationship with this girl for long. We were committed to each other and were about to get married. We even had sex—many times. But then, she cheated on me for another guy and left me.'

'And you want me to lodge an FIR against this girl?' Mishra asked raising an eyebrow. 'FIR for rape?'

'Yes.' I nodded.

'Get up,' he said. There was a sudden change in his tone. It was far from polite.

'A-anything wrong, sir?' I faltered.

'First get up,' he roared this time and walked towards me.

'What is the problem, sir?' I stood up, confused.

'*Saale chutiye,*' he yelled with a power-packed slap on my face. 'What do you think we are here for? To listen to your nonsense?' he screamed again. 'Get out of here.'

And I was thrown out of the police station.

Even the system had betrayed me. I could not believe my luck. Helpless and broken, I dragged myself to the car.

I had just opened the door to get in when I gave up. I was sick of being strong. As I fell on my knees, I screamed like an animal being butchered. 'Bitch . . .!'

If that was not enough to vent out the frustrations and rage I was flooding with, I hit my head against the metal door of car, again and again and again, until a few policemen grabbed me from behind and dragged me away from the car.

~

'You are drunk,' Sub Inspector Baldev Mishra said and gave me a glass of tea. I sat in the same chair where I sat earlier inside the police station. 'Sorry for that slap. We come across so many assholes every day that we are irritated most of the time,' he confessed.

'She cheated on me twice—fucked my emotions,' I muttered.

'I understand. I have a son of your age. Such things are quite common at your age,' he said, politely. The harsh cop was gone. 'But I cannot help you. All I can do is send a constable to drop you home. You are too drunk to drive. Collect your car tomorrow. Go home.'

'I have a friend—Bilal,' I spoke totally avoiding his words, my eyes fixed at the glass of tea. 'He cheated his girlfriend. He promised her marriage and had sex with her, but then, he refused to marry her. They charged him with rape. Can't I file a similar case against this girl?'

The officer laughed.

'I am not joking, sir.' I looked up at him. 'He was charged with rape. I swear. Do you want to talk to him to confirm?'

'You are drunk, boy,' he said. 'Your friend might have been charged with rape under similar circumstances. But that cannot be applied to women.'

'What does that mean?' I was confused.

'As per the Indian law, if a man has sex with a woman after promising marriage—he will have to marry her. If he does not fulfil his promise of marriage after having sex, he can be charged with rape on complaint of the woman. But it is only when the man breaks his promise. This rule is not applied when a woman does something similar to a man.'

'What . . .!' I was shocked. 'You mean a man cannot leave a woman after promising marriage and having sex—but a woman can leave a man? And she won't be punished?'

'Well . . . the law states that.' He nodded.

'Does that even make sense? This is clear gender discrimination. Don't women cheat? I have been cheated on twice by the same girl. What kind of law is this?'

'Well, this is the law. Indian law,' he sighed.

~

It is a fact that strict rules are needed for the protection of women. In a world in which hundreds and thousands of women are molested, raped, mistreated, and even abused in the walls of their own homes by their husbands, strict rules are very important to save them from the evils.

But, how in the world is it justified to punish a man for cheating a woman, but letting a woman go free if she does the same to a man? How is it fair? What if a man is the victim of a woman? What if a man is cheated on by a woman? Does he not deserve justice?

In short, how was Bilal different from Tara? He did to a girl what Tara did to me. Yet, he was charged and punished for rape, but Tara—she was protected by an utterly stupid law!

~

The law failed to provide me justice. But when the law fails—crime is born. The fire to take revenge was still burning deep within me. The hatred for Tara was increasing with every passing minute.

Lost, broken and with hatred in my heart, I reached my home.

'Where were you?' Mom demanded as she opened the door. She visibly relaxed upon seeing me. 'I was calling you all night. You did not even receive my call. At least you should inform me when you are running late.'

I avoided Mom and ran into my bedroom. Without wasting time, I fished an old aluminium suitcase—that once belonged to my grandfather—out of the compartment of my single bed.

And there it was. Wrapped in old newspapers and a wooden box—the revolver that Bilal had gifted me while I was leaving Mumbai.

After shifting to Indore, I realized that it was a mistake to take the gun from him, and thus, I had packed it in the old suitcase and buried it under the bed.

I was wrong. It was not a mistake. I needed it. I needed it today—I thought and loaded the revolver with two bullets. One for Tara—and one for *me*.

I had decided to end it all. I was done with it.

CHAPTER 25

'Is she still here?' I asked Pratyush as I reached his place, and he opened the door. He was fully dressed this time.

'Please let us live in peace, Kunal. She does not love you anymore,' he said, a little enraged. He was slapped.

'Speak as much as I ask you to,' I hissed, pulling the revolver out of my pants. 'Is she still here?'

'Where can she go at this time of night?' He looked scared to death, eyes fixed on the gun, as if he were going to pee his pants. 'I will drop her home in the morning. I p-p-promise,' he slurred.

'Call her out.'

'Tara . . .' he yelled at the bedroom and cowered in a corner. 'You got to calm down, Kunal. You are taking it too far,' he squeaked, eyeing the main door of the flat.

'I have no grudges against you. You can go.' I moved aside to give him some space to run.

That coward asshole did not even take five seconds to run out of the flat.

I walked to the bedroom door as Tara stepped out. She was shaken to see me again. 'Pratyush . . .' she mumbled.

'*Bhaag gaya lodu,*' I laughed humourlessly.

Her eyes widened in fear as she saw the gun in my hand. 'You are sick,' she said in a trembling voice and took a step back, inside the bedroom.

'Am I?' I walked in and closed the door.

'What are you up to?' she screamed.

'The first man you cheated on me for—Ronit—he clicked your nudes and blackmailed you,' I said as I dragged a plastic chair against the door and sat on it. Tara stood as far from me as possible. She was horrified and was trying to find an escape. There was none. 'And the second one left you alone in danger and ran away saving his own ass.' I took a cigarette out of the packet I had purchased on the way to Pratyush's flat. Lighting it, I spoke again, 'Don't you get better men to cheat on me with?'

'I am sorry. I will do as you say,' she cried.

'Tara, Tara, Tara . . .' I breathed. *'Itna chutiya to aaj tak kisi ne nahin banaya mujhe.'*

She leaned against the wall opposite to me, frozen like a statue.

'You want to go? I will let you go. Just give me a satisfying answer,' I spoke grimly. 'Why?'

She stayed mute.

'I mean . . . forget love and all that crap. But didn't you have the humanity to consider the fact that you cheated on me once—and I still loved you? Didn't you have the humanity to consider the fact that I loved you so much that I have your name on my arm with a permanent tattoo? Didn't you have the humanity to consider the fact that I took you to my parents?'

'I am sorry. I just . . . I just didn't feel it for you for the last few days,' she finally replied.

'Alright. Agreed. It happens. Not twice—but it happens. But then, you could have told me. I loved you so much that

I would have let you go.' I paused for a drag. 'But why did you have to jump into bed with someone else when we were still in relationship?' I shouted as I stood up. The chair toppled behind and Tara shrieked with fear.

'I am sorry. Please let me go.'

'Do you remember what you said that day at Bistro Beach when I asked you—what if you cheat again?' I felt the cold revolver in my hand. I was burning with anger, but somehow, I managed to appear calm. Perhaps, because I knew we would be dead in a couple of minutes. Tara and I—both.

'Please let me go, Kunal,' she begged between her heavy sobs.

'You said, "if I ever do—you can kill me,"' I reminded her. 'But don't worry, Tara. You are not dying alone. You will be punished for cheating on me. And I will be punished for letting you do it—the second fucking time.'

My hands trembled as I pointed the muzzle of the gun at her.

As I looked into her eyes for the last time, the memory of the first time I saw her came crashing down on me. It was the first day of the new session at school, and just like previous years, I was in the last bench, talking to Hari, when I happened to glance at the door. That was the moment when a chubby girl with curly hair, having a ring in her nose, walked in. She was nervously looking at her new classmates. I had no idea why, but this girl had all my attention in an instant. She intrigued me. I kept my hand on Hari's mouth to make him quiet and kept staring at her, until our eyes met, and she passed a short, friendly smile at me.

In that moment, however, I never thought that years later I will be standing in front of her—holding a gun in my hand—ready to kill her.

Time. It's a whore.

'Don't do it. Please. I don't want to die,' her voice brought me back to the present.

'No one ever wants to die, Tara—just like no one ever wants to be betrayed, but you see, at times we are left with no choice.' I passed a sadistic smile and placed my finger on the trigger. 'I loved you, Tara. I loved you beyond all limits.' A tear dropped off my eye and I prepared myself to pull the trigger.

EPILOGUE

'You killed her?' Mahesh asked, horrified. He panicked to see blood on my shirt and the gun lying on dashboard of the car.

As promised, Mahesh had taken the first flight in the morning to Indore. If I was unlucky in love, I was damn lucky when it came to friends. We sat in the car right next to the Indore Airport. The crazy night was over, and the golden sunrays were brightening the new day. It was not raining anymore, but the sky was still covered with dark clouds.

'Dammit, did you kill her?' he raised his voice this time.

'I was about to . . . but I did not,' I said.

'Then what about this blood on your shirt?'

'It's my own blood. I guess the stitches broke open,' I said checking my wound and Mahesh relaxed a bit.

'Thank God.' He cleaned his sweat. 'I told you she was a bitch.'

I nodded and lit a cigarette.

'It's anyway not easy to kill someone,' he said again and picked the revolver up from the dashboard and took its bullets out.

'Wrong. In fact, killing someone and committing suicide is very easy. You just have to pull the trigger, and everything ends.' I still had the murderous gleam in my eyes. I could see it in my own reflection. 'The tough part is to control that urge to commit a horrendous crime and choose to stay alive even when life looks pathetically brutal.'

I stooped low in the seat and closed my eyes. Sometimes in life, just some of those rare times, all you need is being empty and to be able to feel nothing but yourself. I guess I was doing the same.

'I know it's hard to get over the first love—but you will definitely forget Tara one day,' Mahesh said in a consoling tone, patting my shoulder.

'Tara was not my first love.' I opened my eyes, turned to face him, and took another drag.

'Fuck . . .!' He laughed. 'She was not?'

'I mean, yes, she was my first girlfriend—but not my first love.'

'Then who was your first love?'

'Some other day,' I said and started the car. I needed to drive. Long drives helped me gain peace of mind.

'I want to know now.' Mahesh pulled the handbrake.

'Alright.' I released the handbrake and took the car on road. 'One fifty kilometres from here, there's a small town—Sendhwa. I spent the initial years of my life in that town. And there I met her, in standard fifth. She was right out my dream—gorgeous and Punjabi. I loved her brown eyes, they were mesmerizing.'

'You remember those eyes yet?'

'Of course—I do.'

'What more do you remember about her?' Mahesh asked. I knew he was indulging me to take my mind off Tara, as that was the need of time indeed.

'Well . . . I remember that day when we were doing rehearsals of a drama for the annual function. The girl who was playing my wife was absent, and as a result, our teacher asked this girl—the one I was mad for—to play the part of my wife just for the rehearsals. And God . . . that was one intense moment when she sat in front of me. She had no idea what was going on in my mind, she just sat there casually. And I just stared. When I looked into those captivating brown eyes, it felt like I had lost my voice. I was so nervous.' I finally smiled. 'I forgot my dialogues, failed to speak anything, and left the rehearsals—blushing like a whore.'

'Blushing like a whore? That does not even make sense,' Mahesh said, laughing heartily now.

'Fuck the words, dude. Concentrate on the emotions, concentrate on the moment.'

'What then?'

'Well, nothing then. She left the school next year and shifted to another. And a year after that, my family shifted to Indore.'

'Did you ever try to contact her?'

'I did send her a request on Facebook.'

'When did you shift to Facebook?' Mahesh asked. 'I guess you love Orkut.'

'I do. But everyone is leaving Orkut and shifting to Facebook,' I said. 'Anyway. The point is—she did not accept my request.'

'Maybe God had better plans for you.'

'Yes. God had. Like getting me fucked by Tara,' I said and applied the brakes.

We stared at each other for a moment. And then, we laughed, and laughed, and laughed, until my eyes went moist. But no, they were not the tears of pain. They were just . . . umm . . . just . . . oh fuck it. It's over.

'So, what now?' Mahesh asked.

'In the game of love, you either play or get played.' I paused to light another cigarette. 'I have been played enough, and now . . .'

'And now?'

'And now I will PLAY.'